SB
_cc-2/13_

WEST POINT OCT 6 1999

RECEIVED

DEC 1 6 1998

BREAK A LEG, DARLINGS

CALAVERAS COUNTY LIBRARY

MH DEC 8 '00

ARNOLD MAY 1 9 2000

ANGELS CAMP OCT 3 2001

COP APR 2 3 '02

MURPHYS NOV 1 3 2002

BREAK A LEG, DARLINGS

Marian Babson

Chivers Press • G.K. Hall & Co.
Bath, England   Thorndike, Maine USA

This Large Print edition is published by Chivers Press, England, and by G.K. Hall & Co., USA.

Published in 1997 in the U.K. by arrangement with HarperCollins Publishers.

Published in 1997 in the U.S. by arrangement with St Martin's Press, Inc.

U.K. Hardcover ISBN 0–7451–8947–4 (Chivers Large Print)
U.S. Softcover ISBN 0–7838–8036–7 (Nightingale Collection Edition)

The text of this Large Print edition is unabridged.
Other aspects of the book may vary from the original edition.

Set in 16 pt. New Times Roman.

Printed in Great Britain on acid-free paper.

British Library Cataloguing in Publication Data available

Library of Congress Cataloging-in-Publication Data

Babson, Marian.
    Break a leg, darlings / Marian Babson.
        p.   cm.
    ISBN 0–7838–8036–7 (lg. print : sc)
    1. Large type books.   I. Title.
[PS3552.A25B74   1997b]
813′.54—dc21

96–49491

CHAPTER ONE

After the fourth murder, I began to notice how hard the seat was. It also seemed to be in two pieces so that, if I shifted incautiously, they moved together in a pincers movement—and I do mean pinch. Repressing a shriek, I ground my teeth together and tried to pay attention to the action on what passed for the stage.

By the eighth murder, I was beginning to be too fed up to worry about professional courtesy—or even ordinary politeness.

'Evangeline'—I tried to keep the whine out of my voice—'Evangeline, can't we leave now? Honestly, I don't feel very well.'

'Shhhh!' She was intent on the figure in the spotlight, who was raising his head like a bloodhound scenting an escaped prisoner as yet another victim moved towards him for the kill.

My heart sank; it was the girl with the terrible scream. Already, I had a throbbing headache from her various demises, each of which she had met with the same high-pitched blood-curdling prolonged shriek. That many decibels should never be let loose in such a confined space. I tried to position my hands unobtrusively near my ears, ready to block out the sound as soon as she opened her mouth.

Farewell, Everyone was strictly a no-budget

1

production. Four actors were playing about twenty-seven parts. (I may have miscounted; the light in here wasn't good and the programme had been typed on a ribbon that had seen its last days long ago, then reproduced on the sort of low-tech, gel-based, clapped-out duplicating equipment that gave car boot sales a bad name.)

The actors were doing their best to ring the changes with varied hairstyles and wigs, different jackets or lack of them for the males, and blouses, ribbons and scarves for the females. They always wore the same shoes, though, so no matter how good the disguise, it was easy to recognize them.

'Why don't I slip out and meet you downstairs in the bar after the show?' I tried again. I could make my move in the fast blackout following the impending murder.

'Shhh!' Evangeline threw me an impatient glance. She couldn't possibly be as interested in the performance as she seemed, but we were in the first row—practically on stage ourselves— and any movement we made would register on the rest of the audience. She turned her attention back to the stage, leaning forward raptly.

This time the girl was wearing a navy-blue smock, grey wig pulled back into a bun and horn-rimmed glasses. She carried a book and brandished it at the man waiting for her.

'According to our records, this book is

thirteen weeks overdue!' Her speaking voice wasn't a great improvement on her scream. 'Furthermore, it has been defaced by a number of nasty reddish-brown stains which were not there when we loaned it to you. Therefore, in addition to your fine for an overdue book, I must charge you—'

The hands lashed out, closing around her throat.

'EEEeeeYYaa—!'

I rammed my fingers into my ears and slid forward in my seat. The instant the lights flickered, I was off.

'No, you don't!' A band of steel closed around my wrist and held me clamped until the lights went on again and I was trapped.

Another actor tottered on wearing another grey wig and carrying a blanket of sewn-together rags in one hand and a large piece of cardboard with stones planted on it in the other. He set the cardboard down so that it became a wall and sat down gingerly in front of it, arranging the rag blanket over his legs. A revolving filter was activated in front of the spotlight and little dots of light fell lazily across the scene, simulating snow. The actor assumed a pathetic expression and began to shiver.

I stifled a moan and closed my eyes. It was at least another fifteen minutes to the interval and I felt as though I had been sitting here for twenty years already. And, judging from the 'cast' list in the programme, there were around

3

seventeen murders still to come.

Sixteen. A cough, a choke and a gurgle from somewhere in front of me denoted that the old beggar had just met some bizarre end—and all without saying a single word. Let's face it, dialogue wasn't a strong point in this production.

Don't ask me what was. The fact that it was taking place in a pub, perhaps. The fact that it was only a short trip downstairs to the bar of the Queen and Country had to be a major factor in its popularity.

I heard another set of footsteps cross the stage and opened one eye to see how much worse it could get. A nun was walking slowly towards the murderer. For a moment, I thought an unlisted member had joined the cast, then I realized that she was wearing black stockings over her shoes, neatly solving the problem of footwear that was much too smart for anyone in Holy Orders. Of course, the trick would only work when long black skirts concealed the tops of the stockings.

The nun was carrying a collecting box. That did it—her fate was sealed.

I wasn't sure just what the playwright's problem was but it was becoming clear that people asking him for money had a great deal to do with it. I began to speculate idly on the possible amount of his alimony payments.

After an eternity of groans, shrieks, grunts, gasps and a strange gurgle I took to indicate garotting, I opened my eyes again to look at my watch. Inevitably, my gaze strayed towards the stage.

The Screamer was in a plain black dress with a white cap and apron, miming an incompetent waitress serving a meal. I poised my fingers over my ears again; I already knew what she was going to get for a tip.

'Evangeline,' I muttered, 'if you don't let me out of here, I swear I'll faint right on the floor.'

'Mmm . . .' Her jaw tightened, but it was only to repress a yawn. 'Perhaps at the interval.'

'The interval,' I agreed, seeing a ray of hope. Once we had navigated those twisting rickety stairs and Evangeline was comfortably settled with a glass in her hand, it would be easy to persuade her that we didn't really want to mountain-climb back up those stairs and we might as well go home.

Abruptly, the Screamer went off and I had to muffle a shriek of my own. Someone had tapped me on the shoulder. Terrified that the performance had turned into an audience-participation venture, I took a deep breath and half turned in my chair to see deep blue eyes in an earnest face regarding me sympathetically.

'I'm sorry to have to tell you this,' he said, 'but there *is* no interval in this play.' Having ruined my evening, he sat back in his chair and returned his attention to the stage.

I closed my eyes and made a mental note to ruin one of Evangeline's evenings some night

5

soon. For the moment, I suspected that *Farewell, Everyone* was doing the job for me. It had been Evangeline's idea to attend this turkey and I wasn't going to let her forget it.

From somewhere at the back, there sounded a shrill titter, quickly stifled, which was a shame. This play might just barely make it if it were presented as a rapid-fire camp comic-strip type of entertainment. Unfortunately, it had been billed as 'A Penetrating Exploration of the Human Condition' and the audience was doing its best to treat the mishmash with the hushed respect it had demanded.

Just another case of everybody believing the publicity, even when directly faced with the contradiction of the actual facts.

'The Emperor has no clothes,' I muttered under my breath.

'And it's not a pretty sight,' Evangeline muttered back.

'*Shhhh!*' somebody hissed sharply. The sound did not appear to have come from behind us. I opened my eyes incredulously, unable to believe that I had actually been shushed from the stage.

The author-star was glaring directly at us, just as the Screamer cut loose again. What a pity if anyone in the audience had missed a decibel of that howl because of our quiet whispers.

'That does it!' Professional courtesy gasped its last. I stood up. 'You can stay to the bitter

6

end, if you want to. I'm bitter enough and I'm leaving now!'

'Not without me, you're not!' Evangeline was on her feet, grasping me firmly under the elbow.

'I'm afraid my friend isn't feeling well.' Cravenly, she threw me to the wolves onstage. The leader of the pack drew back his lips in an unforgiving snarl.

'No, it's all right.' Evangeline waved a dismissive hand in the direction of the informative young man behind us, who was starting out of his chair. 'I can manage perfectly well. She just has these little turns occasionally. I'm used to them.'

'Great!' I muttered as we staggered out into the dim upper vestibule and groped for the railing to those lousy stairs. 'Now everybody thinks I'm some kind of invalid.'

'Next time, you can do the same for me and I'll play ill.'

'What do you mean "next time"? If you think—whoops! Watch it. That step is steeper than the rest.'

'Damn!' Evangeline caught herself just in time. 'I knew it was here somewhere. It tripped me on the way up.'

We were at ground level now and the uneven floor of the Queen and Country stretched out before us. From behind the door marked with an EXIT sign, came the sound of voices and laughter.

7

'I suppose'—Evangeline looked around discontentedly—'there's no way out except through the pub?'

'They get you coming and going,' I agreed. 'I'll bet the takings must be rich after a play like that ends.'

'That's probably why they put it on. After sitting through that playwright's view of society, everyone is going to need a stiff drink.'

Several heads turned as we emerged on the other side of the swinging door and into the bar area. Some of the conversational buzz died down.

'Everything all right, ladies?' The landlord came forward, concerned but not surprised to see us.

'My friend isn't feeling well,' Evangeline told him. 'I'm afraid we had to leave.'

'That's too bad. Can I offer you something?'

'Perhaps a bran—' Evangeline began.

'Not *here*,' I muttered, kicking her sharply on the ankle, perhaps too sharply. She gasped, wincing.

'Are you all right?' The landlord looked frightened, perhaps suspecting some sort of seizure.

'Yes, yes. Just a touch of'—Evangeline glared at me—'my old complaint.'

'Let me get you a drink. My pleasure.'

'I really must get home and lie down,' I said firmly. We wanted to be out of there before the show ended and the cast came downstairs in

8

search of sustenance and praise.

'Thank you just the same.' Evangeline bestowed a gracious smile on him. 'Perhaps another time.'

There was a loud explosion over our heads. We both jumped involuntarily and looked at each other.

'All part of the show, ladies,' the landlord assured us. 'As a matter of fact, it's just as well you left when you did. For the grand finale, he turns a machine gun on the audience. Loaded with blanks, of course, but they don't half make a noise. Deafening, too. I've seen some of the punters take more than an hour to get their hearing back properly. It's a wonder no one has sued him. If he brings down the ceiling some night, I might myself.'

There was another explosion overhead. I saw what the landlord meant. The light fittings shook and the light flickered.

'Home,' I said firmly. 'Now.'

Evangeline nodded and we progressed to the front door, with me remembering to sway a bit while she remembered to limp. We were aware of heads turning surreptitiously to follow our progress.

It was a relief when the door swung shut behind us and we could straighten up and resume our normal gait. As one, we looked about for a taxi.

'Don't give him the address until we're safely inside,' Evangeline warned unnecessarily. We

9

had had too many taxi drivers shake their heads and drive away from us when they discovered we wanted to go to Docklands.

'We should be flat-hunting,' I said. 'First things first.'

'Finding a play *is* the first thing,' Evangeline said. 'Since it is quite obvious that *dear* Hugh has forgotten our existence.'

'We had dinner with them just the other night,' I reminded her.

'And what good did it do us? Did he mention that new play for us? Did he suggest a theatre for us? Did he give any indication that he recognized us as working actors? Did he hell!'

'Give him a break. He and Martha are only just back from their honeymoon.'

'And that's another thing! Those photographs! He bored us for hours thrusting every dreary picture under our noses—even the out-of-focus ones.'

'Some of them were awfully good. Martha looked so happy and the kids were having a wonderful time.'

'Unlike us! Face it, Trixie, we are bereft and abandoned. On our own. Alone!' She sighed tragically and gazed into mid-distance declaiming:

"'Here am I, a stranger and afraid,
  In a world I never made...'"

'Good luck, world!' I muttered, waving
10

frantically at a taxi heading our way with its light on. It veered towards us, slowing, then suddenly lurched back into the lane of traffic and accelerated past us. He had obviously picked us up before.

'We've got to move back to civilization,' I said bitterly. 'No driver ever refused to take us to St John's Wood.'

'Our rent is paid to the end of March,' Evangeline said, in a tone that closed the subject. She looked down the street thoughtfully.

'Here comes another taxi. I'll hail it. As soon as it slows down, you step in front of it until I'm safely inside. Then you get in.'

'Why don't *you* stand in front of it while *I* get in?'

'Because *you* have a dancer's reflexes and muscles. If he tries to drive away, despite your standing in front of him, you can leap on the fender.'

'Oh, thanks a bunch. Why don't I just leap for the roof while I'm about it?'

'As you prefer.' Evangeline moved away from me and waved winsomely at the approaching taxi.

I moved to the edge of the kerb and teetered there. Maybe it would be enough if I just *looked* as though I might fall under the wheels.

There was no need to worry. The taxi drew up smoothly, the driver was beaming at us.

'Here you are, ladies,' he said. 'I thought you

11

might be ready to leave by now.'

'Oh, Eddie, bless you!' We fell into the back seat thankfully. Loud percussive noises began rat-a-tatting through the air behind us, insufficiently muffled by the walls of the Queen and Country.

'He's machine-gunning the audience now,' Evangeline said.

'Good enough for 'em,' Eddie said. 'They want to go to muck like that, serve 'em right. What you want is a nice cheery song-and-dance show, a proper knees-up to send you out happy. Not that stuff.'

'Oh, yes,' I agreed wistfully. 'And something new, please, not one of these endless revivals cluttering up theatres all over town. We saw them the first time round—'

'And didn't think much of them, even then.' Evangeline was critical. 'Silly plots, witless dialogue. Nothing to get your teeth into.'

'Oh, but the music, the melodies,' I sighed. 'They don't write them like that any more.'

'You going straight home, ladies, or are you stopping somewhere for a bit of after-theatre supper first?'

'Home!' We spoke in unison. We weren't going to take our chances on finding another taxi after lingering over a meal. Eddie was the best thing that had happened to us all week.

CHAPTER TWO

Last week hadn't been so good, either. Evangeline had begun agitating for action before Hugh and Martha had even had a chance to unpack their bags. Since they weren't immediately available for nagging, I took the brunt of it.

'Give them a chance,' I protested. 'They've only just got home. They've hardly had time to unpack. And then they've got to get the kids settled in school—'

'Precisely. It is becoming increasingly apparent that we are at the bottom of their list of priorities.'

'You can't say that for certain. They've been in the Caribbean, going to all sorts of shows and getting new ideas. For all you know, they've already discovered a great vehicle for us.' I was getting enthusiastic. I could see myself sashaying across the stage balancing a Carmen Miranda fruit bowl on my head, rolling my hips to the beat of voodoo drums. And it would be typecasting to have Evangeline as the White Witch of Rose Hall.

'And they're taking us to dinner at the Ivy on Friday. Maybe they're going to give us the good news then. Maybe they've found something new and exciting and absolutely terrific for us.'

'Maybe...' Evangeline said, but I could see that my enthusiasm had been contagious. There was a glint of hope in her eyes.

And maybe, some day, I'd learn to keep my big fat mouth shut.

* * *

The dinner was delicious, but the only surprise in store was that there was no surprise at all. It had also long become obvious that Evangeline was not so rapturously enthralled by the photographs of Martha and the children as I was.

'Viola's hair is growing out beautifully and those little curls make her look like a cherub. And I swear Orlando has grown two inches. And, oh Martha, they look so happy.'

'They are.' Hugh took Martha's hand and beamed at me. 'And so am I. Our lives have been transformed. 'And'—he looked into Martha's eyes lovingly—'this is just the beginning.'

Evangeline snorted. Fortunately, they were oblivious, gazing into each other's eyes. This annoyed her more than any curt rejoinder could have done.

'It's wonderful to see Martha so happy,' I said softly to Evangeline, trying to plumb any random maternal instincts that might lie deep below the surface. 'I feel as though there should be violins serenading them...'

14

'A rousing rendition of "Second-Hand Rose" might be appropriate.'

'Evangeline!'

'You can stay here and contemplate Love's Middle-Aged Dream, if you like.' Evangeline pushed back her chair. 'I'm going to go and powder my nose until the dessert arrives.'

No, it had not been an entirely successful evening.

*　　*　　*

Next morning, I was awakened by the familiar sound of breaking china. I reached the kitchen in time to see Evangeline pick up a saucer, take deliberate aim at the far wall and hurl it.

'Now what?' I asked.

'How dare she?' Evangeline picked up another saucer from the pile on the draining board. 'The insolence! The arrogance! How *dare* she?'

I tried not to wince at the crash as the saucer hit the wall. Carefully, I picked my way through the rubble to the kitchen table where Evangeline's half-empty cup of coffee and partially eaten croissant sat neglected. Another saucer hit the wall.

'I see your caffeine fix kicked in early this morning.' I dodged a few flying chips and wondered if I dared cross the line of fire to the coffee pot for my own fix. Eventually, she would tell me what had set her off.

15

Meanwhile, I looked at the morning newspaper beside her plate, still neatly folded and untouched. If there was anything in that to upset her, she hadn't read it yet.

There was also a small pile of letters, some of them addressed to me, I noticed. I picked them up and sorted through, taking out my own. A postcard from Whitby signed by Des and Julian contained only one word I could decipher easily: 'marooned'. I knew just what they meant.

Crash! 'The impertinence!' *Crash!* 'The brass-bound cast-iron nerve!' *Crash!* The pile of saucers was exhausted and Evangeline looked around for something else to throw.

'Anyone I know?' I inquired mildly, taking the opportunity to make a dash for the coffee pot and pour myself a cup. There was no saucer for it, of course, nor little breakfast plate for my croissant. I carried them both across to the table and set them down opposite Evangeline, who had subsided into her chair and was moodily sipping at her coffee. The coffee must be cold by now, but Evangeline was simmering enough for both of them.

'How dare she? How *dare* she? Does she actually expect we'd do such a thing?'

'Who? What?'

Maddeningly, she sipped her coffee, staring into middle distance and shaking her head incredulously.

'Oh, forget it!' I was using the wrong
16

technique, playing into her scene. Now I feigned indifference, ignoring her and picking up a stiff white envelope from my own little stack of mail. I glanced at her from under my eyelids as I opened the envelope and saw that she was watching me with a sardonic smile.

'How nice.' It was an invitation. I glanced at Evangeline again. She was fanning herself with a stiff white card, the twin to my own; her smile had broadened, but was no less sardonic.

'Read it,' she commanded. 'Out loud.'

'What beautiful handwriting.' I was lost in admiration. What wouldn't I give to be able to set pen to paper and get results like that. 'It's what they call copperplate, isn't it?'

'Never mind the form, get to the content.'

'Theatre Royal, Brighton ... pre-West End Tour...' I skipped over the intervening phrases. '... Opening Night Party for ... for *Arsenic and*—' I broke off, choking.

'The sheer effrontery takes your breath away, doesn't it? Inviting us to the premiere of the play she snatched away from under our noses. *Our* play, Trixie. The one *we* should have been opening in.'

Without fully realizing what I was doing, I drained my coffee, stood up—and hurled the cup against the wall.

'Exactly,' Evangeline said with satisfaction. She drained her own cup and handed it to me.

Part of me stood aghast as I snatched the cup from her hand and sent it flying at the wall. I

17

watched the explosion of china shards with disbelief. I couldn't believe I had just done that. I hadn't realized losing the play had upset me so much. Not until Dame Cecile Savoy began rubbing it in.

I took a deep breath and sat down, still quivering with fury.

'Anyway, who cares?' I said defiantly. 'I don't think that play was such a red-hot choice for us. Let her have it. Who wants to play a pair of ancient nutty murderesses? We ought to be able to do better than that.'

'Good thinking, Trixie.' Now that she had me as upset as she was, Evangeline had regained her calm.

'There must be plenty of great vehicles out there somewhere,' I said recklessly. 'And not revivals, either. We just have to find one.'

'You ain't just whistlin' *Dixie!*' We high-fived and then sat back beaming at each other for a few moments before the chill wind of reality swept across us. If there were so many great vehicles out there, why hadn't we heard about them? Why weren't the West End stages swarming with our ageing colleagues showing the younger generation what it was all about?

'Of course, the West End is moribund at the moment,' Evangeline conceded thoughtfully.

'And the musicals are all revivals of shows I didn't even like the first time round,' I agreed.

'And I refuse to play the Nurse in *Romeo and Juliet!*'

18

She might wait until she was asked, but I saw her point. It was the main Shakespearean role producers seemed to consider suitable for actresses who had gently edged over the hill.

'So where does that leave us?'

'Searching...' Evangeline gazed into space with the air of one dedicating herself to a quest for the Holy Grail. 'We must find our own vehicle. Of course,' she came down to earth with a bump, 'that's really Hugh's job. However, since he has either lost interest or is incapable, we shall have to do it ourselves.'

'All right.' Maybe I should have tried to defend my new son-in-law, but I found I more than half agreed with her. Hugh might at least be pretending to get back to business now that the honeymoon was over. On the other hand, it was just remotely possible that he might have been doing something all along and was just waiting until all the details were finalized before telling us. Perhaps there was a script on his desk this very minute...

'I'll talk to Martha,' I said. 'I'll get her to have a look around his office and see if he has anything that might suit us.'

'Martha!' Evangeline snorted. 'Martha is too bound up with those step-brats of hers to see to anything else. Apart from which, she wouldn't know a good script if it leapt out of the pile and bit her on the nose.'

'She would, too. Martha always vetted my scripts for me in Los Angeles.'

19

'And look where that got you! Until you came to England, you hadn't worked in twenty years.'

'Thirteen. And she was right—the scripts I was being offered were terrible. Anyway, you're not counting the voice-overs I did for Tallulah the Tap-Dancing Cat in that cartoon series.'

'I have no intention of dignifying that piece of idiocy by a reply,' Evangeline said severely, in her best Ethel Barrymore mode.

'Meanwhile neither of us is working. Maybe we ought to go to that Brighton premiere and party. We could see what Dame Cecile has got that we haven't got.'

'A producer who's paying attention to business, for one thing.' Evangeline picked up her invitation and began tapping it against the palm of her hand.

'Oh, we'll go, Trixie. We'll go. I wouldn't give her the satisfaction of thinking she's upstaged us. We will go in triumph! With our own show in the offing! And not a mere revival, but a vivid, exciting, brand-new play.'

'Uh-huh? And just how do we accomplish this?'

'We have'—Evangeline checked the invitation—'three weeks. Ample time. Surely we can smoke out an incipient genius in that time. This is London. It swarms with talent.'

'Uh-huh.'

'True, the West End is moribund. We must

20

look farther afield.'

'How about Paris? I could use a bit of light relief.'

'You don't speak French—and neither do I.'

'I was thinking of eating and shopping, not giving speeches.'

'Whereas *I* am thinking of finding a vehicle for us.'

'What's wrong with a nice French farce?'

'We'd have to get it translated before we even knew what we had. And then we might not like it. French always seems to lose a lot in the translation, perhaps because there's nothing much there to begin with. No, Trixie, we want home-grown English-speaking talent.'

'Uh-huh.' But I wasn't being fair. She was right and I ought to show more enthusiasm. 'OK, where do we start, then? There are a lot of provincial repertory theatres—'

'I wasn't thinking of going that far afield,' Evangeline said. 'Not unless it becomes necessary. First, we shall investigate the fringe theatre of London. Quite a lot of original theatre is taking place in pubs these days. We mustn't overlook them.'

'Now you're talking!' My enthusiasm rose. Sitting comfortably in a back room with a drink in my hand as I watched the performance sounded like the sort of luxury that could give watching television at home a run for its money. (How little I knew!)

21

'Yes, Trixie. I was reading a review of a new pub show just last night. Now, where did I put that paper?' She looked around vaguely. 'The review was absolutely glowing. It spoke of a possible West End transfer for the production and the brilliance of the new young playwright. Our search might be over before it starts.'

'Uh-huh.' I knew *that* sounded too good to be true, enthusiasm or not.

'We'll go Monday night!' Evangeline raised her hand as though holding an imaginary champagne glass. I responded with one of mine. Even in my imagination, I could see a crack appear as the glasses clinked together.

'That reminds me'—I looked at the pile of shards at the foot of the far wall—'we'd better do some shopping. We need more crockery.'

'Good! I could do with a trip to Harrods.'

'Actually, I was thinking of one of those wholesalers who supply Greek restaurants.'

CHAPTER THREE

And so we staggered home from our first excursion into pub theatre, bloody but unbowed. It couldn't all be like that. Could it?

'That obviously was not our sort of place.' Evangeline flung her coat over the back of a chair and headed for the brandy decanter. 'Nor did I like the way some of those people looked

22

at us. One felt that they were up to no good.'

'Sinister as all get-out,' I agreed half-heartedly. They had seemed perfectly ordinary people to me. If an eyebrow or two had been raised and a few glances exchanged as we walked through the saloon bar it was probably because they weren't accustomed to seeing members of the audience walking out in the middle of a performance. Or it could have been that we'd lasted longer than they thought we would. We were well above the average age of most of the audience.

On the other hand, there was always the possibility that they had recognized us. In which case, perhaps it was unfortunate that we had overdone the staggering bit in our anxiety to escape without being too insulting to the performers.

'There are plenty more pub theatres.' Evangeline handed me my drink 'We'll make a list and cover them one by one.'

'If that show got such good reviews'—I took a deep swallow and shuddered—'what are the others like? The ones that got bad reviews?'

'Only a fool pays any attention to reviews! We shall form our own opinions untrammelled by prejudices or preconceptions.' She sipped at her brandy and stared thoughtfully into space. 'Once we get through our list, which will start with those on the verge of closing, we can concentrate on openings, where there'll be no chance of any other viewpoint influencing

23

our own.'

'Uh-huh.' This was beginning to sound like a long haul. I didn't bother to stifle my yawn.

'Now where ...?' Evangeline looked around, still bright-eyed and bushy-tailed. 'Where did I put that listings magazine?'

'You make your list.' I yawned again and headed for my bedroom. 'I'm calling it a night.'

*   *   *

It was as well I got a good night's sleep. Evangeline was already seated at the kitchen table when I got up. A closely scribbled sheet of paper was in front of her and I did not feel that it boded well to find her poring over the *A–Z Atlas of London*. I had already suspected that most of the fringe venues were going to be located a long way from the West End.

'I've arranged the possibilities in the order of their closing.' She greeted me without looking up. 'We'll have to toss a coin for tonight; it's the last night for two of them. They don't seem to run for very long,' she added on a note of complaint.

'That should tell you something right there.' I poured a cup of coffee and rummaged in the breadbox, settling for a slightly stale poppy-seed roll. With butter and jam, it would do.

The small stack of mail at my place did not look very exciting: a couple of obvious advertisements, another plaintive postcard

24

from Julian and an unidentifiable envelope with French stamps, which had been readdressed from the St John's Wood house.

I picked it up curiously. No, no, I didn't recognize the handwriting but, somehow, I didn't like the vibes it was giving off. I began to remember what curiosity had done to the cat. Still, it was addressed to me and I couldn't not open it, could I?

Gingerly, I inserted a finger into the little ungummed space at the end of the flap and began to work it open. A cloying sickly sweet scent made my nose wrinkle. I held the envelope a little farther away from me and eased the letter out, unfolding it and scanning the signature.

'Good Lord! Sweetums!' I yelped.

Evangeline reared back. She looked over her shoulder and then all around the room. Nobody there but us chickens. She glared across at me.

'You were not, I trust, addressing me?'

'Certainly not! It's from Sweetums. Sweetums Carew!' Incautiously, I flapped the letter at her. A great gust of heliotrope eddied out, engulfing us both and setting us gagging. Sweetums often had that effect. 'Surely you remember her.'

'Sweetums!' Evangeline choked, in the tone people usually reserve for violent oaths. 'I'd hoped she was dead.'

That was another familiar reaction to Sweetums.

25

'Oh, come on,' I said. 'She's not that bad. Not really.'

'What does she want?' Evangeline demanded icily.

It was a good question. No one had ever heard from Sweetums unless she wanted something from them. I looked for the answer.

'Here it is.' Halfway down the page, after a totally insincere couple of paragraphs about what good pals we had always been and her delight at hearing such wonderful news about us. 'She's arriving in London, uh ... soon ... and is dying to see us again.'

'She's heard we're doing well and wants to horn in on it,' Evangeline translated. 'How did she find us? How did she get our address?'

'She's been on part of a world cruise. The Fort Lauderdale to Acapulco leg. Beau and Juanita were on board; they gave her all our news. But she used the old address, the letter has been forwarded. Beau can't know that Jasper lost the house yet.'

'Jasper has a lot to answer for,' Evangeline said darkly. 'And so does Beau. *When* did you say she's arriving?'

'Well, er...' She wasn't going to like this.

'Don't shilly-shally, Trixie. When?'

'Um...' I looked at her grim face, but there was no use in trying to keep it from her. 'Today, in fact.'

'Today. Sweetums Carew.' Evangeline rose

to her feet. 'I find I have a blinding headache. I am going to bed for the rest of the day, perhaps the rest of the week.'

'What about all those plays we need to see?' That halted her halfway to the door. She changed course and came back and poured herself another cup of coffee instead.

'We might always hope—' She carried it back to the table and sat sipping it thoughtfully. 'We might always hope that she'll go to the old address and there'll be no one there to redirect her.'

'We might, but I wouldn't take any bets on it.'

'I suppose it *would* be too much to hope for,' she agreed. 'We'll have to think of other ways to protect ourselves.'

'Evangeline—' I didn't trust the faint half-smile quirking her lips. 'Promise me you'll be nice to her.'

'Why should I be?'

'Well . . .' The only reason I could think of was a negative one. 'She hasn't done anything nasty to us . . . lately.'

'Only because she hasn't had the chance.'

That was true enough to silence me. It was awfully hard to defend Sweetums Carew. Of course, most people outside the business didn't know there was anything wrong with her; they believed all that sweetness and light she projected. Considering the way things are now, it's really amazing to look back on those early

27

innocent days of fan magazines, gossip columnists and publicity handouts and realize how tightly the studios were able to keep the lid on everything.

Oh, Hedda or Louella regularly revealed exciting scoops with much fanfare, but the really nasty damaging revelation stayed firmly buried—except for the occasional murder or scandal that erupted in the public press and law courts too violently to be hushed up. There were enough of those to convince the public that it knew everything about the stars and almost everything about the featured players. Walter and Jimmy could be tougher, especially if they took a dislike to someone but, basically, the stories were of the Jack Benny-who-pretends-to-be-a-miser-is-really-the-first-one-to-grab-the-check-at-any-restaurant-and-refuses-to-let-anyone-else-pay sort. They never reported items like Beauregard Sylvester, who gave the impression of being an open-handed big-hearted Joe, still having ninety cents out of the first dollar he ever earned and being so vain yet sneaky that he had sent his wife to test out a new face-lift technique before he tried it himself. Nor, when the experiment had gone disastrously wrong, did they break the story. Oh, no. They weaselled out with touching little yarns about Juanita retiring from the screen to devote herself to her husband and children and enjoy sweet domesticity.

So, although most of them knew a few unsavoury anecdotes about Sweetums, it was a lead-pipe cinch nobody was going to print them. Not after Sweetums sent a box of chocolates, with live tarantulas alternating with chocolates in the top layer, to the gossip columnist who had hinted at her less-than-sweet disposition. Sweetums had never believed in letting the studio publicity department fight her battles for her.

'*That's why ... the lady is a tramp...*' Humming under her breath, Evangeline was riffling through the pages of the pub theatre listings. I watched uneasily; I didn't trust that smile.

'What are you up to now?'

'Just revising tonight's programme. I will not allow that ... creature ... across my threshold, so we'll invite her to the theatre with us.'

'That sounds reasonable.' Too reasonable for Evangeline. I watched her closely.

'Here we are!' She found what she was looking for and beamed at the page. 'At the Red Bull tonight: Maxim Gorky's *The Lower Depths*. Sweetums should feel right at home there.'

'Maybe, but what about us?' I winced at the idea of sitting through that. 'The last I heard, Gorky wasn't in any position to accept a commission to write a new play for us.'

'We'll just have to sacrifice tonight to the

29

prospect of getting Sweetums out of our hair. If she thinks we're into that sort of theatre, she won't be so anxious to hang around with us.'

'Good point.' I tested out a couple of earnest intent expressions. 'Do you think she'll believe it?'

'If she doesn't...' Evangeline scanned the listings. '*Phèdre*, in the original French, is playing at the Bijou Theatre by the Green tomorrow night.'

'At least it won't lose in the translation.' I had a sudden dire thought. 'Maybe Sweetums speaks French, that letter was mailed from Paris.'

'French has nothing to do with it,' Evangeline said. 'Sweetums could always get her own way in any language.'

'Couldn't she just!' There was a moment of silence as we contemplated the truth of that. Single-handedly, Sweetums had been responsible for six heart attacks, four automobile crashes, several strange accidents to co-workers, innumerable nervous breakdowns and at least one suspected suicide. And those were just the incidents we knew had been hushed up.

'Poor Cuddles,' Evangeline sighed. 'Thank heavens he was able to escape before it was too late.'

I nodded. S. Z. (Cuddles) Sakall, flustered, lovable and cuddly, and Sweetums Carew, fluttery, feminine and adorable, had seemed

30

like perfect pairing for a series of low-budget but highly bankable 'B' pictures. On paper, it was casting made in heaven; when they got on the set together all hell broke loose.

Nobody was going to be cuter, cuddlier or more adorable than Sweetums, even if she had to kill them to keep her title. The director was carried off with a heart attack and subsequently changed his career path to become a market gardener ('Vegetables,' he had said later, 'give you no back talk'), two cameramen and the script girl had nervous breakdowns and the writing team took off for the Fiji Islands where they settled down to writing novels. The picture was written off and the series shelved.

Apart from a tendency to break into shakes and wring his cheeks with both hands whenever Sweetums's name was mentioned, Cuddles got away relatively lightly. Needless to say, they never worked together again. Each reigned supreme as the most adorable character in subsequent separate pictures.

'Sweetums, after all these years,' Evangeline said. 'How did she survive when so many nicer people have bitten the dust? It just goes to show, it's the green bay tree all over again.'

The telephone rang and we both cringed. Somehow, we knew it couldn't be anyone else. I stood up reluctantly.

'Tell her to meet us at the Red Bull,' Evangeline said, a scheming glint in her eyes.

31

'We'll eat there before the performance. The menu looks absolutely disgusting.'

* * *

'Well, I must say!' Sweetums fluttered eyelashes that were a quarter of an inch too long for belief, or even comfort, and looked from Evangeline to me. 'You girls have certainly changed. In your tastes, that is. Not otherwise, of course. You still don't look a day over sixty, just the way you were when I first knew you, all those years ago. I can still remember how awed I was. Little me, meeting such important actresses, and so much older ones.' She looked around. 'There's a strange background noise in this place, isn't there?'

Actually, it was Evangeline's teeth grinding, but I thought I'd better not point this out. I wouldn't give Sweetums the satisfaction of thinking she was annoying us.

'Something to do with the darts game, maybe,' I suggested. There was a lively game going on in one corner. In another corner, a group of young men huddled together and seemed to be paying a certain amount of covert attention to us.

'Oooh!' Sweetums followed my gaze and simpered at the men. 'Don't look now, girls, but I think we've been recognized.'

'They're probably wondering who the old freak is,' Evangeline muttered.

32

'Oh, you don't look that bad.' Sweetums had heard it. 'Just terribly exhausted and rather distraught. Are you sure you haven't had a nervous breakdown recently?'

'Any minute now,' Evangeline threatened, clenching one hand into a fist.

'Why don't we order?' I tried to distract them, waving the gravy-stained piece of cardboard that served as a menu to be shared among the three of us.

'I'm not very hungry.' Sweetums wrinkled her nose, then simpered when she realized the men were still watching.

'But you must try some English specialities.' Evangeline took the menu from me and surveyed it. 'There's a Ploughman's Platter, Bubble-and-Squeak, Toad-in-the-Hole...' Her voice faltered and I knew how she felt. I wouldn't trust this place not to serve up a real toad.

'I'll just have a glass of white wine,' Sweetums said firmly. 'I'm sure we can find a decent place to eat after the show.'

'I'll have a lager and crackers and cheese,' Evangeline decided.

'Sounds safe—I mean, good—to me,' I agreed. If Sweetums wasn't going to risk her digestion on any of the menu selections, neither should we. Furthermore, the reek of heliotrope surrounding us had killed any appetite I might have had.

The waiter was looking at us rather oddly

33

and with a certain amount of displeasure. Obviously he had hoped for a more impressive order—in which case, he should have had a more impressive menu.

'Don't look now'—Sweetums rolled her eyes and prinked at her hair—'but I do believe we're going to be asked for our autographs.'

Sure enough, one of the young men had detached himself from the group and was heading purposefully towards us, a scrap of paper in his hand.

Automatically, we arched our necks, tilted our heads to the most becoming angle, and smiled.

'Oh!' Sweetums gave a pretty start, raising her hands and widening her eyes, at discovering him at her side.

'Miss Carew?'

'Oh, please, call me Sweetums,' she simpered, turning the full force of her saccharinity upon him.

'Er...' And they hadn't even been introduced. The tips of his ears glowed red and he retreated a nervous half-step. 'Yes. Thank you ... Swee—' He could not bring himself to do it. 'Miss Carew.'

'And you're Miss Sinclair?' He turned to Evangeline with visible relief; she was not going to invite him into undue familiarity.

'Was there any doubt?' Evangeline froze him with her best Ethel Barrymore glare. He shuffled a step sideways and turned to me.

34

'And Miss Dolan?'

'Yes?' By this time, I wasn't prepared to be any more welcoming. I had had time to notice that the scrap of paper he clutched was filled with cramped writing and scribbled figures; there was no room on it for any autographs. So, what *did* he want? I raised an eyebrow and waited.

'Great honour to have you here, to meet you,' he said earnestly. Why didn't I believe him?

'Like to buy you a drink. All the pleasure you've given. In your time. My gran was a great admirer. Never missed one of your pictures. All of you.' He was getting in deeper with every stumbling word. Even Sweetums had stopped smirking.

'Anything you like.' He ground the words out from between clenched teeth, increasingly nervous in the face of our silence. He glanced back over his shoulder at his friends across the room. A couple of them made encouraging gestures.

'Name your pleasure,' he invited recklessly.

Evangeline looked thoughtfully into the distance. Hanging-drawing-and-quartering him would be her pleasure at this moment.

For perhaps the only time in her life, Sweetums's mask had dropped enough to suggest that she was in complete agreement.

'Thank you.' I broke the silence. 'I'm afraid we haven't time. The performance is due to start. We'd better get upstairs.'

'Afterwards, then.' He was pale but determined, perhaps he thought we might be in a more amenable mood after we'd survived the rigours of the performance.

'I think not.' Evangeline bared her teeth at him, sending him back another step before he caught himself. She hadn't missed those friends of his in the background waiting to rush forward and join the party the minute we showed any signs of letting down the social bars. 'We have had more than our quota for the evening—' She indicated her half-empty lager glass with an expression that implied she had reached the outer limits of her endurance. The idea of a sip of anything stronger ever having passed those untainted lips was unthinkable.

'Oh. Of course. Of course. Perhaps next time. Are you coming to the next presentation? *Mother Courage*. It's the start of our Bertolt Brecht Season. Followed by *Umberto Ui*. We're all very excited about it.'

'Oh, yes!' I managed to sound wildly enthusiastic and was glad to see that Sweetums looked distinctly as though she was having second thoughts about linking up with us— even if we were successfully reviving our careers. Some prices were too high to pay.

'How thrilling!' Evangeline repressed a shudder and glanced at Sweetums, who was now visibly shrinking in horror at the prospect.

'We wouldn't dream of missing it!'

'Good. Great.' He waved a hand in our general direction and, flushed by the prospect of escaping him I actually caught it and shook it. He appeared overwhelmed. 'Oh, Miss Dolan!'

A buzzer sounded and people at surrounding tables began lurching to their feet, grabbing their glasses and heading for a narrow door at the far end of the room.

'I'm not sure I can stay.' Sweetums was on her feet and baulking; 'I don't think I feel too well. Jet lag, you know.'

'Nonsense!' Evangeline seized her elbow in a steely grasp. 'You had plenty of time to get over your jet lag in Paris. You'll love the show. You'd never forgive yourself if you missed it.' Relentlessly, she urged Sweetums forward.

'Well.' I tried to free my hand without turning it into a wrestling match. 'It's been nice to meet you, um...'

'Vic,' he said earnestly, gazing into my eyes but still not releasing my hands. Our moment of pressing-the-flesh seemed to have unnerved him completely. He pulled me closer, clasping my hand to his heart. 'Victor Varney, at your service.' He made it sound as though he had just won a tournament and declared me his Queen of Love and Beauty. I was touched— but I still wanted my hand back.

The buzzer sounded again and a second wave of delinquents pushed back their chairs

37

and made for the staircase. Evangeline and Sweetums were at the door; Evangeline looked back and signalled to me.

'I must go.' I tugged my hand free; he released it reluctantly.

'Next time,' he said.

I smiled, not sure what I seemed to be agreeing, and hurried to catch up with the others. When I looked back over my shoulder, I saw that Vic Varney had returned to his group of friends and seemed to be arguing furiously with them. The scrap of paper was taken from him almost forcibly and someone began adding more notes to it.

'Hurry up.' Evangeline tried to sound enthusiastic. 'We don't want to be late for the performance.'

Sweetums muttered something under her breath; it didn't sound sweet at all.

CHAPTER FOUR

In the morning, I stood at the telephone, not bothering to keep a straight face as Sweetums earnestly explained that she had been smitten by a strange malady during the night. The symptoms included dizziness, aching limbs, spots before the eyes and many other unspecified discomforts, all of which meant that she would not be able to join us on this evening's theatrical excursion.

'Oh, what a pity,' I sympathized. 'I know you would have loved it. One so rarely has the opportunity to see an Urdu company presenting the uncut five-hour version of *The Decade of the Maharishi*.'

'Oh, I'm utterly *devastated* at the thought of missing it,' Sweetums assured me. 'But I'm afraid I'm going to be out of action for some time. I can tell it's just terribly serious. I'm sure no reliable doctor would allow me out at night for at least a week. Maybe longer.'

'How rotten for you.'

'Yes. I was so looking forward to sharing the intellectual life of London with you girls. Last night was ... memorable.'

'Never mind. You just concentrate on taking care of yourself and getting well. 'Bye now.' I replaced the receiver as Evangeline entered the living room.

'It worked,' I reported. 'Sweetums is off our backs. Some mystery virus has laid her low, probably for the remainder of her stay. And we did it all first crack off the bat.'

'Thank heavens for that! We can go back to the A List now and see some decent shows.'

'Uh-huh.' I cocked an eyebrow at her. If she thought that, she'd obviously forgotten what we had already seen and what was on offer. I'd heard of the triumph of hope over experience, but this was ridiculous.

'Here we are.' Oblivious, Evangeline

discarded one sheet of paper and concentrated on the other. 'Tonight is the closing night of *Flying in the Face* ... at the Happy Larry.'

'Face of what?' It sounded highly suspect.

'Oh ... tradition, I suppose. Or danger. What does it matter? "A frothy delight",' she began quoting from the scribble beside the title. 'It must be a comedy.'

'I'll believe that when I see it.'

'And,' she added cunningly, 'the pub is in Islington. That's this side of the West End. Not so far to travel. If we start out in time, we can make bus connections all the way and see some new territory.'

'Oh, all right.' I gave in. 'I suppose we might as well.'

* * *

Islington is on the other side of town from St John's Wood, so we had never explored it before. It turned out to be a lively upbeat area with lots of restaurants, pub theatres, shops, street markets, an antique centre, a cinema, and crowds of people thronging it all.

Since we got there in plenty of time, we browsed through a few antique shops and had an early dinner at an Italian restaurant before going on to the Happy Larry for the show.

It did seem to be a happy pub. We entered into a buzz of conversation and laughter which seemed to wrap around us and welcome us.

40

Tables were crowded and there was a jam at the bar. We looked around with approval; this was more like it. Maybe there was hope for the show yet.

'Oh, look, Trixie,' Evangeline carolled suddenly. 'There's that nice Superintendent Who-He!'

I followed her pointing finger and couldn't believe my eyes. There, indeed, was Superintendent Heyhoe—as we had never seen him. Standing at the bar in jeans, T-shirt and denim jacket, talking with several men who seemed to belong in this ambience. An explanation abruptly came to me.

'Shhh, Evangeline!' I nudged her quickly. 'He must be doing undercover work. Don't give him away!'

Too late. The little group had looked up and spotted us. Superintendent Heyhoe flinched visibly as Evangeline bore down on him, beaming.

'Good evening, ladies,' he said through clenched teeth. 'Who's dead now?'

'I don't know,' Evangeline said brightly. 'Who?'

'Someone must be,' he said. 'You're here.'

'There's a theatre upstairs,' I reminded him coldly. 'We've come to see the show.'

'You promise?' A faint hope seemed to dawn at the back of his eyes, but he was still mistrusting. 'That's your only reason?'

'Of course. But what are *you* doing here?'

41

Evangeline ignored another nudge. 'And dressed like *that?*'

'I'm off duty, madam,' Heyhoe said stiffly. 'And I live in this neighbourhood. This happens to be my local.'

'That's right,' one of the men said. 'A copper off duty is just as good as anybody else. He even has friends.'

I wasn't so sure about that. Now that a couple of the men at the fringes of the group had turned away and were talking to other people there was a new lightness in their bearing, a relaxation they hadn't displayed when talking to Heyhoe. He was not the only one mistrustful around here. The defectors kept casting curious little sidelong glances at us. Either they had recognized us, or they thought we were up to something, or both. In any case, they were content to step aside and leave Heyhoe to deal with us.

'Of course he has friends,' Evangeline said warmly. 'And we're happy to count ourselves among them.'

Heyhoe didn't look happy at all. He checked his watch. It was getting close to performance time.

'Aren't you going to introduce us, Ron?' his friend prompted.

'Ron!' Evangeline breathed triumphantly.

Glowering at her, Heyhoe mumbled the introductions. His friend's name was Barry Lane.

42

'Pleasure and honour, ladies,' Barry assured us. 'Can I get you a drink?'

'They don't have time,' Heyhoe said quickly. 'There goes the warning bell.' A sharp peal underlined his words.

'Perhaps at the interval,' Evangeline said graciously. 'If you'll still be here?'

'I'm not sure—' Heyhoe began.

''Course he will,' his friend interrupted. 'His wife's gone to the country, so he's making a night of it.'

'Wife?' Evangeline was enchanted, she was learning far more than we had ever known about Heyhoe. Of course, we had never seen him in a social context before.

'Have you got your tickets yet?' Heyhoe's shoulders hunched defensively as he tried to hurry us off. He didn't want to get into any social context with us. I suppose I really couldn't blame him considering...

'We booked by telephone,' Evangeline said. 'Where do we pick up our tickets?' We both looked around vaguely.

'Upstairs, at the door,' Barry said. 'Good job you booked. Last night of a very popular show. Full house every night. We may bring it back for a return engagement later on. But there's a new show coming in next week. You'll like that, too.'

'I'm sure we shall.' Evangeline beamed at him, but I was still looking around and I had lost my own smile.

'Evangeline,' I said. 'Look. Who's. Here.'

Evangeline turned slowly and was just in time to see Sweetums Carew consolidate her Grand Entrance with a flourish of the handsome young man on her arm. A faint scent of heliotrope wafted through the room; on the whole, I preferred the cigarette smoke.

'Oh!' Sweetums was scanning the room to see if she was making enough of an impression and saw us. She was not pleased. That made three of us.

'Hello, Sweetums,' Evangeline greeted her. 'Feeling better?'

'Oh, yes. Yes, thank you. How lovely to see you girls again. And so soon.'

'Just what we were thinking,' I said. We looked at the handsome young man escorting her. We were thinking a lot more than that.

'Oh, yes,' Sweetums simpered, correctly interpreting our main point of interest. 'You haven't met my dear Terence, have you? He came to the hotel this morning, just in time to rescue me from the depths of despair. I was feeling terrible, coming down with whatever dreadful virus was in the air, when the telephone rang—and *he* was downstairs! Wanting to see me! He's President of the Magnificent Stars Fan Club.'

'Magnificent Stars of Yesteryear Fan Club,' Terence corrected in an undertone. He'd better watch his step. The look Sweetums shot him suggested that he was one chocolate away from

44

a rendezvous with a tarantula.

'*Magnificent Stars*,' she emphasized, squeezing his arm so hard that he winced.

'I explained that I had the most frightful headache,' she continued. 'So he began stroking my forehead and gave me the most wonderful neck massage! Terence has healing hands!'

'Uh-huh.' Evangeline and I spoke in unison. We carefully refrained from looking at each other.

'Then I felt *so* much better'—Sweetums fluttered her improbable eyelashes at Terence—'that I thought I *could* manage a show tonight. Terence told me this was *the* one to see, especially as it was closing tonight. And so, here we are!'

'We heard that, too,' Evangeline said mendaciously. 'So we changed our plans at the very last moment and came here. What a coincidence.'

'We'd better get upstairs,' I said, as the final bell rang. 'The show is starting.'

'Oh, no need to hurry.' Barry Lane beamed at us. 'We can hold the curtain for a few more minutes, if you'd like a drink or anything.'

'How kind of you,' Evangeline said. This time, we did allow our glances to meet swiftly. There was no mistaking the sudden authority in his voice. Barry Lane was not just a drinking mate of Superintendent Heyhoe, the unmistakable accents of Mine Host rang in his voice. He was unquestionably the person in command of the pub and, quite probably, the theatre, too.

'Lane...' Evangeline mused thoughtfully. 'One of the Lupino Lane family, I presume.'

'Well, at some distance,' he acknowledged. 'But, yes, one of the clan.'

'Kissing cousins!' Sweetums trilled prettily. 'I should have guessed you were in the Profession. You have that look about you.'

'Oh, no,' he disclaimed hastily. 'The divine spark passed me by, but I've still got all the instincts. I make my living from the pub and I indulge my hobby and creative instincts by maintaining the theatre upstairs. It's quietly gaining a not inconsiderable reputation, I'm happy to say.'

Somewhere along the way, he had waved his hand to some effect and an ice bucket containing a magnum of champagne had materialized beside us.

'Plenty of time for a quick one,' he said. 'The players will be glad of an extra few minutes to get themselves together. Most of them have a day job and they can use a bit more time to catch their breath.'

He was expertly twiddling the cork and, catching and correctly interpreting Terence's anxious look, said hastily, 'All on the house. My pleasure, ladies. You too, Ron.' He hadn't missed Superintendent Heyhoe's attempt to withdraw. 'Stay and keep your friends company.'

46

'Ah, yes.' Heyhoe was not quite sure that he wanted to keep company with us, but he was beginning to relax a bit. After all, he was off duty, so why shouldn't we honestly be about our own concerns? Possibly it was sheer fluke that we had been involved in such unhappy circumstances in the past. 'Thanks, Barry.'

I smiled reassuringly at him and he almost smiled back.

'A toast—' Barry filled the glasses briskly, including one for himself, and stepped back, holding his glass aloft.

'To the fairest flowers the cinema has ever known,' he said. 'It's an honour to have you gracing my establishment this memorable evening. Now that you've found your way here, I hope you'll make this your local and come often.'

Heyhoe twitched, but managed to force a smile and sip from his glass. After all, he knew where we lived and how far it would be to come. There was precious little chance of our making the Happy Larry our local.

A rhythmic stamping of feet began overhead. The rest of the audience wasn't happy at the delay.

'Oh, how lovely,' Sweetums sighed, turning her languishing gaze on Barry. 'You are so kind, so gentlemanly. You make me feel so happy and so at home here.'

I felt the enamel on my teeth begin to
47

disintegrate. Sweetums ought to carry a dental health warning; exposure to her could result in cavities. Or, as one director had rashly noted (just before he lost his job), Sweetums was so sweet she could melt the enamel off your teeth—while she was stealing your gold fillings.

'You must come again.' Barry fell for it, hook, line and sinker. 'Our next show will start on Tuesday. I'll arrange tickets for all of you.'

A bell sounded loudly and angrily, brooking no insubordination.

'Umm, yes.' Barry looked thoughtful. 'Perhaps you ought to get upstairs. It sounds as though they're ready to start.'

It sounded as though they had been ready for the last half-hour, but we smiled and emptied our glasses.

'Ooooh! Those stairs are so steep!' Sweetums squealed. 'How lucky I am to have a man with such a strong arm to cling to!'

Evangeline ground her teeth and, disdaining the stair-rail, marched straight up them. I followed, but took the precaution of using the stair-rail; those stairs *were* awfully steep and I didn't intend to take foolish chances just because Sweetums had goaded me into it. Not that the stair-rail was anything to depend on, it felt distinctly wobbly.

At the top of the stairs, Sweetums swayed against Terence, giggling. Thrown off balance, Terence stumbled. They teetered at the top of the stairs, looking as though they might crash

48

down to the bottom at any second. Sweetums stopped giggling and gave a panic-stricken shriek.

Evangeline thoughtfully moved over to one side of the staircase to allow them free clearance if they did fall.

Then Terence recovered his balance, gave Sweetums a shove, and they were safely away from the head of the stairs and any further peril.

The girl at the ticket desk waved us all through, another girl led us to two pairs of empty seats—a good distance away from each other, thank heavens—and the lights went down as soon as we had settled ourselves.

*　　*　　*

At least it was a cheerful show. Juvenile, but cheerful. A great improvement over the last ones we had seen, but it didn't really hold any promise for us.

I was more discouraged than Evangeline. She returned from the ladies' room with her eyes gleaming and her nose twitching at a new scent.

'There were some young girls in there talking about a fantastic new Irish poet,' she said. 'We've got to check him out.'

'I don't really think a verse play is us,' I protested.

'Undoubtedly, he will be able to write prose

49

as well, if he's that good.'

'If . . .'

'Think of Yeats,' she urged. 'Think of Synge. There's no reason why we might not be in on the start of a great career.'

'Uh-huh.'

'I've got the address. He's appearing at the Green Colleen in Kilburn. We'll go tomorrow night.'

CHAPTER FIVE

The Green Colleen was an Irish pub straight out of Central Casting. Shamrocks featured heavily in the decorating scheme and there was even a wizened crone smoking a clay pipe. Instinctively, I looked round for Barry Fitzgerald, who should be twinkling by the bar.

'What do they do for an encore?' I murmured to Evangeline, but she was too busy inhaling the atmosphere to pay any attention. It looked all right to her.

'Oh, yes,' she breathed. 'Yes, this will make a wonderful stage set.'

'If you ask me, it already is.'

'Excuse me—?' Evangeline wasn't going to ask me anything, she was directing her query to the man behind the bar. 'Where is the performance tonight? And when does it start?'

50

'Right here, as ever was.' He beamed on her. 'As soon as Himself gets here.'

'Ah, it's Finn you're wanting to see.' The man who came up behind us was too tall and too thin to be Barry Fitzgerald, even in his younger days, but he was doing his best. 'A great fellow. A towering giant of a talent. You're right to come here to see him, he's the best thing in town, even if say it myself who's been his best friend these twenty-eight years.'

'I'll have a brandy.' I didn't believe him, either. He was a stage Irishman in a stage pub. 'How about you, Evangeline?'

'Yes, yes.' She brushed me aside, intent on cosying-up to the best friend of the talent. 'Tell me, does your friend write anything besides poetry?'

'You name it,' he said expansively. 'He writes it.' Where had I heard that before?

'There you are.' The bartender set glasses down on the counter in front of me, expertly tweaking the ten-pound note from my fingers. I saw that a pint of Guinness had joined the brandies and divined that this was the price of rubbing shoulders with genius at one remove.

'Very kind of you.' Our new-found friend took possession of the pint and raised it to us. 'Shall we bag a table before they all fill up?' He started to lead the way; following him, I tripped.

'Careful, now.' He turned back. 'Don't trample on The Semtex.'

51

Evangeline gave a muffled shriek, then looked annoyed as several people within earshot burst into laughter.

'Oh-ho, it gets them every time!' our friend chortled to his cohorts. 'Mind The Semtex—we don't want any explosions. Not unplanned ones.' There was fresh mirth from all concerned.

I followed his proud gaze. An enormous grey Irish wolfhound was stretched out full length on his stomach. I had stumbled over his gigantic front paws.

'That's Semtex?' I asked.

'*The* Semtex,' he corrected. 'Oh, we have a fine time with him, I can tell you. Every time the police bust the place, we say, "Oh, yes, The Semtex is over there. Mind you don't jar it, we won't be responsible." Of course, the lads from the local nick are all on to that one now, but every once in a while we get fresh meat from the Anti-Terrorist Squad and they fall for it every time.'

The wolfhound opened his large mournful eyes and rolled them resignedly at the man. It was the most world-weary animal I had ever seen. He had heard it all before and was in mortal danger of expiring from sheer boredom. Its IQ was probably about twenty points above that of anyone else in the place. Evangeline and myself excepted, of course.

'Tell me...' On second thoughts, I wasn't so sure about Evangeline. She took a seat and

52

cooed at the man. 'What *is* your name?'

'Brendan Mahoney.' He sketched a bow. 'At your service. And I know who you two are. I'm just surprised it took you so long to find your way over here. You've a treat in store tonight.'

'I'm sure we have,' Evangeline cooed again.

'Although, mind you'—he frowned judiciously—'I've taken the precaution of putting us at a table near the door. It's strong meat, ladies, very strong. It might be too much for your delicate sensitivities. Why, we had a young girl in here the other night who fainted. Mind you, she was straight out of convent school in the Old Country.'

I began to wonder what we had let ourselves in for.

'No, I doubt you'll faint,' Brendan decided. 'But no one will hold it against you if you find it too much and wish to slip out quietly.'

The saloon bar was filling up rapidly now. The crowd seemed to be mostly Irish, although they were advertising their rebellious spirits by the number of rings they displayed in ears, noses and who knows where else.

'The poet seems to have a big following,' I remarked.

'He does that. His fame is growing by leaps and bounds. I tell you, the day is coming when Dorsal Finn will be a name to be reckoned with.'

'Dorsal?' Evangeline repeated incredulously. '*Dorsal* Finn?'

'Sure, his mother had a great sense of humour. Always laughing and making jokes. Lots of the babies were being named Declan that year, but she wanted something different. When he was good, as a lad, she called him Dor; when she didn't like what he was doing, she called him Sal. Oh, she was the life and soul of the village. Always cheering people up. Funny, Finn should grow up to be a bit of a misery.'

A tall, rangy, saturnine figure strode through the swinging doors just then, followed by a horde of handmaidens. He nodded sourly to Brendan and walked straight to the bar. The bartender automatically set a glass of Guinness down in front of him. He grasped it firmly, backed off a few long strides, then rushed forward and leaped to the counter top without spilling a drop. The audience erupted into violent applause.

'Just like dear Errol,' Evangeline breathed. 'Although he'd have emptied the glass before he landed.'

I glanced at her sharply. I had always wondered about that time when she'd co-starred with Errol Flynn. Some very interesting rumours had been flying around.

The poet gazed down at his audience impassively, then took a deep swallow, emptying half the glass. This set them off again.

'Enough!' He silenced them with a wave of

54

his glass. 'We have not come here to have a good time. We have serious business to discuss.'

My heart sank, but Evangeline remained hopeful. 'Good stage presence,' she murmured approvingly.

'We are here to address the state of our nation,' he declaimed, 'and a sorry state it is. We have let the world use us as a theme park, but the times are changing—they have to change—and the world doesn't realize it yet.'

The Semtex gave a long woofling sigh and hunched himself together to take up as little space as possible. He looked longingly at the door.

'So I've prepared my own State of the Nation Report—and a Warning Shot across the bows of the World! The first item is:

Leprechauns Aren't What They Used To Be
The leprechauns have strapped on guns
They'll ram-raid the rainbow.
Fuck the crock of gold!
They're after the pool of blood
To drink, drink deep.
It will make them strong.
Not human, just strong.
Increase their sperm count
So they can rape the virgin colleens
And the nine-month fruit
Will drop into the pool of blood,
Not human, but strong

55

Fit to live and kill
In this bloody land.
The leprechauns are on the rampage!
No longer mischievous,
But vicious.
The fairy gold glitters and disappears,
The Uzi and the bullets remain.
They are real,
They are the legacy.
The blood runs into pools...'

'I have a headache,' Evangeline announced.
'And it's getting worse with every stanza.'

'We don't have to hang around,' I agreed sotto voce, stealing a look at Brendan, who appeared enraptured. 'There's nothing here for us.' Since he had deliberately seated us near the escape hatch, Brendan would understand—or think he did. I just hated to have him think we were leaving because it was too much 'strong meat' for us. It was just plain awful.

'The legends lie...' Dorsal Finn was still at it. He changed his stance for another poem. The bartender passed another pint of Guinness up to him. 'Here is the truth:

The Legends Lie
Kathleen Mavourneen's on the game,
Mother Machree is her pimp,
The Minstrel Boy runs the brothel,
Last one in is a wimp!'

56

'Speaking for myself,' Evangeline surged to her feet, 'I intend to be the first one out.'

'You and me both.' I was right behind her. It was clear that I was not going to be deprived of a great cultural experience if I never heard the rest of that little gem.

Brendan nodded understandingly as we left. The Semtex stared after us enviously.

The irate poet raised his voice to follow after us:

'Gomorrah, begorra!
Not a saint in sight...'

By that time, we were out of sight, too. The doors swung shut behind us, cutting off his voice. We walked down to the corner of the street without looking back, breathing in the cool damp air thankfully.

'Yeats, he isn't.' Evangeline took a deep breath. 'Nor Synge, nor Wilde.'

'Closer to the Behan boys, if anything,' I said. 'But not close enough.'

The momentum of freedom had carried us along but, at the corner, Evangeline stopped abruptly. 'Where are we?' she demanded.

'God knows.' I looked around. Between the small oases of light that marked the pubs, there were lots of shuttered shops and windows covered with tattered posters. Vague figures drifted past or, in several cases, staggered past. The place seemed more sinister in the darkness than it had in the earlier twilight. Or perhaps it was the after effects of that miserable poetry.

In any case, this was beginning to look like a good place to get away from. The night was dark and we were far from home.

'Do you suppose there's such a thing as a taxi rank around here?' Evangeline was looking increasingly unhappy.

'I'm a stranger here myself, but I wouldn't bet on it.'

We both stared hopefully down the deserted street. Suddenly, there wasn't any traffic at all. It was getting colder, too. It even seemed to be getting darker. The lights in a shop window behind us flickered and went out.

'There!' Evangeline pointed dramatically into the distance. 'There comes one!'

'It may already be hired.' I squinted at the slowly approaching vehicle. 'The light on top is out.'

'More probably coming home for the night, in this area.' She watched it keenly, prepared to give no quarter. 'Get the door open and get inside before we tell him where we want to go. He has to take us, once we're inside.'

'I know.' I sighed faintly. If only we still lived within a decent distance of the West End, we wouldn't need to resort to these subterfuges. 'He's going to be furious.'

'Would you rather stand here all night?'

I sighed again and braced myself. She was right. Better to face the wrath of a taxi driver

58

than to wander around here for hours. And we *did* tip well.

Amazingly, the taxi slowed and veered towards us, giving every indication that it was going to stop in response to our frantic waving.

'Maybe our luck has changed,' I said optimistically. 'It's not such a bad night, after all.'

'Get inside first,' Evangeline said grimly. 'Before he can change his mind.' She seemed to be breathing heavily, almost panting, as we waited for the taxi to draw up in front of us.

'Relax,' I said. 'He's going to stop. See?'

True to my words, the taxi slid up alongside the kerb and came to a halt.

'Quick!' Evangeline commanded.

I wrenched the door open and we tumbled inside.

'You needn't push!' Evangeline snapped.

'*You* pushed *me*.' But my rejoinder was abstracted. There had been something about the taxi door, something I had half glimpsed in my anxiety to open it and get inside . . . I looked at the driver, but a reversed baseball cap turned head and neck into a distorted amorphous blur . . .

'EEEEK!' Evangeline shrieked as a large hairy body hurtled into the taxi before I could close the door behind us. 'Help! Muggers!'

She began striking out at the hulking figure looming over us. 'Get out! Get out of here!'

'Beat it!' I slammed at it with my handbag,

59

but it stood firm.

'You ladies need help?' the driver asked.

'Drive straight to the police station,' Evangeline instructed. 'We'll see about this!'

I pushed at the dark hairy form again, but couldn't budge it. The door slammed shut as the driver took off at high speed. The figure lurched against me. There seemed to be an awful lot of hair. Evangeline was panting heavily again. Or was she?

'Ye gods!' Realization suddenly came to me. 'It's The Semtex!'

'What?' the driver squawked. The taxi swerved wildly.

'Not that kind,' I said. 'It's a dog.'

'Stop right now!' Evangeline ordered. 'Throw that thing out of here!'

'He must have followed us out of the pub.' I felt some sympathy for him. 'That poetry was too much for him, too.'

'What's going on back there?' the driver demanded. There was something oddly familiar about that voice. 'I thought I could trust you two not to be any trouble.'

'We'll be all right as soon as we get rid of this monster,' Evangeline said.

'Poor thing.' I gave him a tentative pat. 'Imagine having to listen to that stuff all night every night.'

'You can't keep him, Trixie. Take him back immediately.'

'Me? I'm not going back into that joint

again. Suppose *you* take him back.'

The taxi had pulled up under a streetlamp at the kerb on the opposite side of the road now and the driver twisted around to peer into the back seat. 'What's going on back there?'

'Nothing.' Evangeline took advantage of the stop to open the door. 'You've got an extra passenger, that's all. We're getting rid of him now.' She pushed at The Semtex, who promptly sat down in front of her.

'Help me push him out, Trixie. Both together now. One ... two ... three!'

We heaved at him. We might as well have tried to topple the Rock of Gibraltar.

'Put your back into it, Trixie!' Naturally, it was my fault. 'Again: one ... two ... *three!*'

The Semtex wuffled happily at this new game and slumped forward to lie full length on the floor, his tail sweeping it enthusiastically.

'It's no use,' I said. 'He's bigger than both of us.'

'Out, sir! Out, I say!' Evangeline used the voice that had turned countless villains into cringing wrecks before the stern wrath of her outraged purity. 'Out! Out! Out!'

The Semtex licked her ankles, which was more than any of the villains had done. On screen, at least.

'Can I help?' The driver had left his post and come round to the open door. In the light from the streetlamp, I got my first good look at him ... her. The situation had lacked only this.

61

'Evangeline!' My voice was a strangled croak. 'Look! It's Nova!'

'Nova!' Evangeline actually sounded pleased. 'What are you doing here?'

'Driving through. We live just beyond here. Wasn't that lucky? Great to see you two again. We've gone past the house a few times, but there's never been any sign of you. We thought we'd lost you.'

'We've been filming in Whitby,' I said quickly.

'And now we're back and looking for a new play to star in.' Evangeline let it all hang out. For a moment, I wished The Semtex would bite her. 'How is dear Lucy—and what is she working on these days?'

'Wait till you hear—you'll love it! But I won't spoil her surprise by telling you about it. Right now, she's got a job. She's working as assistant stage manager at the Emperor Uncloth'd. Of course, she's really doing all the work. The director is supposed to be stage manager, too, but he isn't pulling his weight at all. Lucy is lumbered with everything.'

'Poor dear,' Evangeline cooed. 'But I'm sure she's coping admirably. *And* she's keeping up with her own work, too. I can't wait to hear all about it.'

'Meanwhile,' I tried to interject a note of reality, 'do you think you can help us get this ... this creature ... out of the cab? He belongs back there at the Green Colleen. He followed us. We didn't encourage him. We didn't even know he was there.'

'Sure.' Nova hooked her hand into the beast's collar and tugged. He lowered his head and the collar slipped over it. Nova staggered back and only just kept her balance.

'That didn't work,' Evangeline noted unnecessarily. 'Perhaps if we put the collar back on. Tighter. And tried again.'

'Not too tight,' I protested. 'We don't want to throttle him.'

'Why not?' Evangeline's voice was cold. 'We want to get this nuisance out of here and go home.'

The nuisance slobbered over her ankles again. She winced fastidiously and moved them away.

'All right.' It had become a duel of wills between the two of them. Evangeline braced herself against the back of the seat and planted both feet on the animal's rump. 'Come on, Trixie—push! Nova—pull! One ... two ... *three!*'

Our concerted efforts failed to budge him. In fact, they seemed to be doing him a world of good. He had lost his world-weary air and was almost puppylike. He whinnied happily, delighted at being the centre of so much attention.

'It's no good,' I said. 'One of us will have to go back to the pub and get somebody to come and fetch him.' I knew there was no use looking

63

at Evangeline, so I looked hopefully at Nova. So did Evangeline.

'That pub's got an odd reputation.' Nova was unexpectedly as skittish as one of those newly escaped convent school girls Brendan had been telling us about. 'Let's keep trying. Once we get him out of the cab, he'll find his own way home. He has nowhere else to go.'

Oh, hadn't he? The Semtex seemed to have formed his own opinion about that. He dropped his enormous head between his forepaws and went to sleep.

'We can't stay here all night,' Evangeline said fretfully.

I silently agreed. Sitting in the taxi was marginally better than standing on a street corner, but I was increasingly anxious to get back to the comfort of what passed for home these days. Never mind the location, the call of a well-stocked fridge and bar, central heating, a hot bath and a soft bed was irresistible.

'Never mind the dog.' I just managed to keep the whine out of my voice. 'I want to go home.'

'We both do.' Losing patience, Evangeline kicked at The Semtex. He twitched, but remained otherwise unmoved.

'Look—' Nova slammed the door on us and went back to her perch. 'Leave it to me. I'll drive you two to St John's Wood—it isn't far from here. Then I'll bring the dog back and get one of the blokes from the pub to see to him.'

'Ummm...' That opened a different can of

64

beans. Evangeline and I crossed glances briefly. She averted her gaze and kicked pettishly at The Semtex again. It was up to me.

'The thing is,' I said, 'we don't live in St John's Wood any more. We've, um, moved farther out.'

'How far?' Nova was instantly—and justifiably—suspicious.

'Well, um, we're in Docklands now.'

'Docklands!' The motor roared and died. 'What are you doing *there?*'

'It's a long story,' I said, 'but we didn't have any choice in the matter. Believe me, we're longing to get back to civilization.'

'I should think so.' Still the motor stayed silent. 'Look, I'm sorry, but I don't think I can take you there.'

'You've got to!' Desperation made Evangeline savage. 'We're in your taxi.'

'It's not a real taxi,' I reminded her. Too late, I remembered that it was the 'Widows' Might' logo I had partially noted on the cab door as I had opened it. 'This is a private vehicle.'

'It's not that,' Nova said earnestly. 'I'd take you, if I could. The thing is'—she hung her head—'I'm afraid I haven't got enough petrol to go that far.'

'Is that the only problem?' Evangeline relaxed. 'Don't worry about that. We'll pay for the petrol.'

'We'll *fill* the tank.' I glared at Evangeline, challenging her to deny it.

65

'Oh, you don't have to do that.' Nova sounded a lot more cheerful. 'Although, of course, I *will* have to come all the way back here with the dog...'

'We insist,' I said firmly. 'It's the least we can do.'

CHAPTER SIX

Back at the block of flats, it appeared that The Semtex still had ideas of his own. He was the first one out of the taxi as the door opened. He loped over to the lamp post across the road and relieved himself mightily, then he bounded up the steps and stood waiting for us, his tail wagging madly.

'This isn't going to be as easy as it sounded back in Kilburn,' I muttered.

'Damn!' Evangeline glared at The Semtex and drew herself up to her full height, gesturing imperiously towards the still-open cab door.

'Get *in*, sir!' she commanded. '*In*, I say! Get in!'

The Semtex cocked his head, looking puzzled.

'You're confusing him,' I said. 'First, he was in the cab and you kept telling him to get out. Now he's out and you're telling him to get in.'

'Here, boy!' Nova got out and came round to stand beside us. 'Here! Come on!' she whistled hopefully.

The Semtex wagged his tail and looked up at the door behind him. He was willing to go in, but into the building, not the taxi.

'Here!' Evangeline trumpeted. 'Come here, sir!'

The Semtex turned his back on us, his attention obviously caught by something going on in the entrance hall.

'Someone's coming.' Evangeline started forward, divining the situation instantly. 'Don't let him in!' she called.

Too late. Nigel opened the front door and was nearly knocked off his feet as The Semtex charged past him.

'Now you've done it!' Evangeline flung at him accusingly, as we all rushed in.

'What was that?' Nigel stood there bemused, staring at The Semtex as it did a brief canter around the front hall, then headed for the staircase.

'An Irish wolfhound.' I paused to answer while Evangeline and Nova continued in pursuit.

'You're sure it wasn't the Hound of the Baskervilles?' Nigel gazed at the now deserted staircase as though unwilling to believe his eyes.

'Are you all right?'

'I think I have a couple of broken toes.' Nigel looked down at his feet gloomily. 'That—*thing*—not only stepped on them, he ground down on them to get purchase for his leap across the hall. Didn't Jasper tell you pets aren't allowed? It's in the lease.'

'We don't have a lease,' I reminded him. 'And it's not a pet—at least, not our pet. It just followed us—'

'Stop!' ... 'Grab him!' ...

There was a hullabaloo above us, shrieks and cries intermingled with excited yelps. The Semtex appeared at the top of the stairs, then skittered down them with joyful yaps. He was having a wonderful time with his new playmates. This was a lot more fun than lying around a smoky pub listening to dreary poetry.

'Watch out!' Nigel pulled me back against the wall. 'He's coming this way.'

The Semtex bounded up to us and stood there, panting happily.

'Go away!' Nigel whined. 'Get lost! Shoo!'

The Semtex gave a pleased yelp. Another new pal. He reared up on his hind legs and put his forepaws on Nigel's shoulders.

'Get away!' Nigel buckled at the knees. 'You weigh a ton!' He tried to avoid the affectionate tongue aimed at his face.

'Hold on to him!' Evangeline bellowed from the top of the stairs; she began descending at a much slower pace than The Semtex. 'Don't let him get away again.'

'Open the door, Trixie,' Nova directed, overtaking Evangeline and passing her. 'Then nip ahead and open the cab door for us.'

68

'You—' She indicated Nigel. 'Pick him up and carry him out to the car.'

'Pick him up?' Nigel echoed weakly. He was slowly sinking to the floor under the weight of The Semtex. 'Carry him? Are you mad?'

Just to show willing, I opened the door.

'I'll help you.' Nova advanced on them. 'You take his head and front legs, I'll take the hind legs.' She heaved at the dog's hindquarters, his claws scrabbled frantically against the polished marble floor as she tugged, then he tilted forward, hind legs off the floor, his full weight on Nigel.

They all teetered perilously for a moment, then abruptly collapsed in a heap.

'I don't think this is going to work,' Evangeline announced. She had reached the bottom of the staircase now and was standing there regarding them judiciously.

The Semtex struggled to the top of the heap and sprawled across Nigel and Nova, watching Evangeline happily. He obviously considered her Mistress of the Revels and he thoroughly approved. This was a lot better than a bar-room brawl and not nearly so dangerous.

'Maybe you'd like to suggest something better.' Nova sounded perilously close to mutiny.

'Trixie, go upstairs and get a piece of steak from the fridge. We can lure him into the taxi with it.'

'I suppose it's worth a try.' I crossed to the

69

express lift and pressed the call button. The lift was there and waiting; the doors opened smoothly. I stepped inside and pressed the button for the penthouse. The doors began to close again.

There was a frantic yowl, a wild skitter of claws across marble and The Semtex hurled himself through the closing doors and skidded to a stop just short of colliding with the opposite side of the lift. He sat down, his tail thumping heavily against the floor, shaking the lift as we ascended.

'Oh, no!' I wailed. 'No!' There wasn't a thing I could do about it. The doors were closed and we were gliding relentlessly upwards.

Thump-thump-thump. The lift cage shook.

'Don't *do* that!' This lift was temperamental enough at the best of times. It wouldn't take much to throw it into one of its fits of noncooperation. I didn't want to be stuck in the lift shaft with The Semtex all night.

'Sit,' I pleaded. 'Just sit quietly. We'll be there in a minute and then—' And then what?

Thump-thump-thump. The Semtex watched me expectantly. Even sitting down, he was nearly as tall as I was. *Thump-thump-thump.*

'Stay!' The lift was slowing to a halt. 'No! Sit! Stay! Please, stay! Just wait here and I'll go and get the steak.'

The lift doors slid open and The Semtex rushed past me into the little foyer we shared with the other penthouse apartments. With

70

him in it, it seemed to shrink to doll-house proportions.

He raised his nose and sniffed the air, then went unerringly to our door and down in front of it, waiting for me to open it. I heard the hum of the other lift approaching. Reinforcements, I hoped.

'There!' Evangeline came out fighting. 'I knew it! Why did you let him into the lift with you? And, if you had to, why didn't you keep him in there?'

'If you think it's so easy...' I smiled sweetly at her. '*You* try it!'

'Have you tried luring him with the steak?' Nigel was right behind her with his helpful suggestion.

'I haven't had time. We just got here. And what are you doing here? I thought you were on your way out. That's how he got inside in the first place.'

'I'm only trying to help.' Nigel gave me an injured look. 'I was only going out for a bit of exercise. A short walk and perhaps a quick one at the pub. Changing plans won't exactly ruin my evening.'

In fact, this might make his evening. There was a gleam of anticipation in his eyes. It would not only make a great anecdote to impress future clients with, but he might even get a free drink or two out of it.

'You'll get exercise all right if you're going to tangle with that mutt,' Nova grumbled, 'but

71

can we hurry it up? I'm sorry, but I can't hang around here all night. I have to pick Lucy up at the pub after the show.'

'Go get the steak, Trixie.' Evangeline twined her fingers lightly into the dog's collar. 'We'll keep him here.'

'Sure.' This I had to see.

I turned the key in the lock and The Semtex surged to his feet.

'Quickly, Trixie.' Evangeline tightened her grip. 'Just open the door enough to slide throu—'

The door flew out of my hands, the hairy body hurtled past me. Evangeline lost her grip and lay sprawled across the threshold.

'Why didn't you stop him?' she demanded. 'Why didn't you?'

The Semtex skidded to a stop in the middle of the living room and whirled to face us with a yelp of triumph.

'Here.' Nigel gave Evangeline his hand and hoisted her to her feet while I started for the kitchen. I was aware of loud thumping footsteps behind me. Pawsteps? Pawfalls? Whatever, I was being followed by The Semtex.

'We might as well have a drink.' Evangeline and the others were also right behind me. 'We've earned it.'

'What a good idea,' Nigel approved.

'Not for me, thanks,' Nova said quickly. 'I'm driving. And I ought to be on my way. If we can't get that beast downstairs and into my cab, I'm going to have to leave him here.'

We all turned and looked at The Semtex. He had slumped down in front of the fridge and stretched out to his full length. He looked back at us and yawned, then let his head drop on to his forepaws and closed his eyes.

'It looks like he's settled for the night.' I stated the obvious.

'Big, isn't he?' Nigel eyed him thoughtfully. 'Heavy, too,' he remembered. 'I don't think he's going to move again until he wants to move.'

'No, you're not going to shift him again tonight.' Nova glanced at her watch. 'I'd better get going.'

'Maybe we can telephone the Green Colleen and get somebody there to come and collect him.' As soon as I said it, I began having second thoughts.

'I think not.' Evangeline raised an eyebrow at me and I knew what she was thinking.

'You can't do that.' Even Nova could see the drawbacks in the idea. 'You don't want all those weirdos to know where you live.'

'No, no, we don't want that.' Nigel glanced over his shoulder nervously, as though the shadow of the bailiffs flickered amidst the other shadows in the corners of the room. 'We have enough weird characters around here now.'

I nodded agreement, trying to avoid a

pointed look at Nova. It was probably too much to hope that she would go away quietly and forget where we were living these days.

'Look,' Nova said. 'I hate to leave you in the lurch like this, but I've got to pick up Lucy. Why don't we both come over tomorrow morning and ferry the hound back to Kilburn for you?'

'That sounds like a good idea,' Evangeline said. 'If you think we'll be any more successful at moving him then.'

'Don't worry,' Nova said. 'By morning, he'll be wanting to see that lamp post again. When you get him outside, just don't let him back into the building. Then, when you get into the taxi, he'll follow you again, the way he did tonight.'

We all looked thoughtfully at The Semtex, who appeared to be out for the count. There was no way we were going to budge him again tonight.

'That's settled, then.' Nova started for the door. 'We'll see you in the morning.'

'Not too early,' I put in hastily.

'No, no. Around eleven. And then—' She looked at Evangeline the way The Semtex might look at a nice juicy T-bone steak. 'Then Lucy can tell you all about the new play she's writing.'

'Quick, Nigel!' I sank wearily into a chair as the door closed behind Nova. 'Start pouring the drinks.'

*   *   *

Evangeline's scream woke me in the morning. I rushed out into the kitchen to find her face down on the floor in front of the fridge. The fridge door was open and The Semtex had his hind legs planted firmly in the small of her back while he burrowed into the depths of the fridge, helping himself to breakfast.

'Get him off me!' Evangeline squirmed convulsively, trying to slither out from under the massive paws. 'Kick him! Slam the door on his head!'

'Uh-huh.' I advanced cautiously, ignoring her suicidal commands. I didn't think it would be a good idea to get between The Semtex and his food. Technically, of course, it was our food—but I wasn't prepared to argue the point with him.

'Don't just stand there!' Evangeline snapped. 'Help me!'

'OK, OK, I'm trying.' I watched The Semtex, gauging my moment. He was unaware of anything except the food. Something slid and crashed in the fridge. The Semtex lunged forward after it, raising one hind paw to scrabble against the bottom shelf.

'Quick!' I gave Evangeline my hand and pulled. 'Roll out from under.' Cursing, she did so.

'There.' I got her to her feet. 'All right now?'

75

'No thanks to you!' She glared at me. 'What took you so long? I'll be bruised for weeks from those paws.'

'I suppose you opened the fridge door for him.' A counterattack was the only way to deal with Evangeline when she was in this mood.

'I did *not* open the door for him. I opened it for myself. I was planning to get some breakfast.'

'So was I, but we can forget about that idea.' We watched gloomily as The Semtex withdrew from the fridge, licking his chops. The inside looked like a war-devastated area. Only a lone container of crème fraîche was relatively intact.

The Semtex turned to follow our gaze, noticed the container, pawed it out on to the floor, knocked the lid off and slurped up the crème fraîche.

'Well,' I said, 'at least we don't have to worry about what to feed him. Thank goodness you didn't open the freezer.'

'Too bad I didn't,' Evangeline said. 'A couple of broken teeth might have taught him a lesson.'

'*Rrrrufff!*' The Semtex shook himself and looked at us expectantly. When we didn't respond, he cocked his head, then loped around the kitchen sniffing at the legs of the tables and chairs. I got the nervous feeling that his head wasn't the only thing he was going to cock in another minute.

76

'Evangeline,' I said. 'I think he's looking for that lamp post.'

'That wouldn't surprise me. You'd better get dressed and take him downstairs.'

'Me? Why don't you do it?' I didn't really expect an answer and I didn't get one. 'Anyway,' I continued, 'I can't take him down. We haven't got a leash for him. Suppose he runs away?'

'In that case, I should say we were ahead of the game.' Evangeline looked at the dog coldly. He had been negotiating an approach to the table leg, but he caught her look and backed away uneasily. 'You'd better hurry,' she added, 'or you'll have an awful mess to clean up.'

'Well, come down with me,' I bargained. 'It must be nearly time for Nova and Lucy to arrive. The four of us ought to be able to herd him into the taxi. And then maybe we can go somewhere for breakfast; there's nothing left for us here.'

'Oh, all right.' As she passed the fridge, Evangeline vented her feelings by slamming the door on the denuded shelves. As an afterthought, she turned back to the dog.

'SIT!' she thundered.

The surprised animal collapsed as though his legs had turned to jelly. I had seen her have the same effect on some of the toughest directors and actors of our time.

'We'll be right back,' I said. 'Just stay there.'

77

The beast whined piteously, thankful for a moderately kind word. His gaze followed Evangeline as she left the room. I didn't worry him quite so much.

In my bedroom, I had an idea and rummaged in the wastebasket for the ruined tights I had discarded the night before. They would have to double as a leash while we took the dog back to his owner. They might be unsightly, but they would be effective.

CHAPTER SEVEN

We were waiting for the lift when the door to an opposite penthouse opened and Jasper and Mariah came into the foyer.

'Oh, good. I'm glad I've caught you.' But Jasper did not look pleased to see us. Nervously, I moved in front of The Semtex, although hiding him was about as likely as Jimmy Durante trying to hide his following elephant in *Jumbo*. Nor did I think the famous riposte, '*What elephant?*' would cut much ice with Jasper. As Nigel had informed us, pets were banned from the premises.

'We were just coming to call on you,' Mariah said. 'Another minute and we would have missed you.' She sounded as though she regretted not having lingered for another cup of coffee.

78

'Oh, really?' Evangeline had caught the intonation, too. She eyed the pair dismissively. 'We're in a hurry, I'm afraid.'

'Oh, quite. Quite,' Jasper said apologetically. 'This will only take a minute ... a minute ...' He trailed off, obviously unable to bring himself to the point. This was going to take a lot longer than a minute—and The Semtex was already starting to sniff at the legs of the foyer table.

The hum of the approaching lift grew louder and we both edged closer to the doors. We were in no mood for any more of Jasper's angst. Mariah was helping him with his problems—she should be enough.

'No, wait. Please.' He stepped in front of us as the lift doors slid open. 'I've *got* to talk to you. It's impor—' He broke off as The Semtex lunged for the opening, nearly knocking him over.

'Good God! What's that?' He stared incredulously at the dog.

'Haven't you ever seen an Irish wolfhound before?' Evangeline asked crossly, trying to sidestep him and get into the lift.

'You're sure it's not the Hound of the Baskervilles?'

'We laughed the first time at that one,' I said. 'But not very much.' The lift doors jittered indecisively, then began sliding shut again. The Semtex gave another piteous whine.

'He's very big,' Mariah said in a small voice.

79

It struck me that she was afraid of dogs, but making a brave effort. 'What's his name?'

'The—uh—' I stopped and crossed glances with Evangeline. The poor mutt had enough strikes against him without continuing to be saddled with that ridiculous name.

'Tex,' I said firmly. 'His name is Tex. Isn't it, Tex?'

The wolfhound, recognizing at least the last syllable of a familiar sound, wagged his tail and wuffled a friendly agreement.

'Tex. Hello, Tex.' Mariah drew a deep breath and held out her hand. The newly christened Tex sniffed at it and wagged his tail again. He turned his head to me approvingly, obviously feeling that he was meeting a better class of people these days.

'Tex...' Jasper frowned unhappily, the name seemed to remind him of something, perhaps several of his grandfather's famous roles.

'He's not ours,' I said quickly, before Jasper could get the wrong idea. 'We were just, uh, keeping him for a friend last night. He's going back to his owner now.'

'Never mind that.' Jasper waved a hand, dismissing all lesser problems. 'I must talk to you. I ... I need your help. Please.'

'What's wrong?' Evangeline asked sharply.

'They're coming back. Early! They're almost here. They rang from Paris last night. They want me to meet them at Heathrow. What am I

80

going to do?'

'Meet them, of course.' Mariah patted his arm consolingly. 'Don't worry. It will be all right.'

'You don't know them.' Jasper would not be comforted. 'And *they* don't know. They're expecting to be taken to St John's Wood for a few days before they go home. How can I tell them?'

'How about the same way you told us?' Evangeline was not prepared to be gracious about it. 'Cold turkey. The shock will do them good. Get the old adrenaline flowing.' She reached out to push the lift button and reopen the doors.

'No, please.' He caught her hand.

'You mean Beau and Juanita have come back?' Light was beginning to dawn. Nothing less would upset Jasper so much. Or terrify him so much. 'Their cruise is over already?'

'They've cut it short, for some reason.' He was ashen-faced. 'You don't suppose they've heard anything?' He shook his head dazedly. 'Please, you've got to help me.'

'What did you have in mind?' Evangeline asked warily.

'I—' He brightened. 'I suppose you wouldn't be willing to meet them at the airport?'

'You're right,' Evangeline dashed his hopes. 'We wouldn't.'

'Oh, please. You know them, you can talk to them, make them understand.' His voice

81

broke, his chin quivered.

Evangeline turned away impatiently. She hates to see a grown man cry—unless she's the cause of it.

'It will be all right,' Mariah assured him. 'I'm going with you. We'll drive them to a nice pub in the country for lunch and explain everything.'

'You've never met them,' he said brokenly. 'My grandfather—' He could not continue.

'His grandfather still has the first dollar he ever earned,' Evangeline informed her crisply. 'He gave new meaning to the word "tight". There were rumours that Jack Benny's scriptwriters used Beau for a model. He hates to spend money and could never understand people who wasted it. He disapproves of speculations; all of his investments are gilt-edged.'

Jasper let out a low moan. Mariah looked shaken.

'I don't blame you for being afraid to face him. You won't have an easy time of it.' The thought appeared to cheer Evangeline. 'People have been disinherited for less.'

Jasper moaned again.

'Jasper wasn't irresponsible,' Mariah defended quickly. 'The project should have been successful. No one could have foreseen the way the economy was going to crash.'

'No one who hadn't lived through 1929,' Evangeline said. 'Unfortunately for Jasper,

Beau still has nightmares about that. It was the closest escape of his life. He was a teenage success on Broadway and had actually been considering buying some stock at that time. Happily, it took so long to bring himself to part with the money that the crash came first.'

Jasper began to shake. If Evangeline didn't stop, she was going to give him a nervous breakdown before Beau had a chance to take a crack at him.

'Easy, Jasper, easy,' Mariah soothed. 'He can't be that bad. Between us, we should be able to make him see reason.'

'My grandfather? Reason?' Jasper gave a bleak hollow laugh.

'He has a point,' Evangeline said. 'The best advice I can give you is to concentrate on Juanita, then let her work on Beau. If anyone can bring him round, she can. And Jasper is her favourite grandchild.'

'I'm her only grandchild,' Jasper moaned. 'And I've let them both down.'

'Only in the short term,' Mariah said. 'Once we get this place finished and the rest of the flats built and sold, long term it will show a profit.'

In about a hundred years, maybe. I wondered what Beau's opinion would be of that. However, I had no doubt about one of his opinions.

'Beau will approve of you,' I told Mariah. 'He's crazy about people who know how to

83

make numbers work. In fact, they're about the only people he respects. And you've been doing a great job here.'

Single-handedly, Mariah had been snatching our leftover Yuppies from the jaws of the Bankruptcy Courts. Much of what she had done was as mysterious to me as it was to them, but I was vaguely aware of meetings with banks and sundry creditors and rescheduling of debt payments and curtailments of credit cards. Mainly, I was aware of a growing lightness of spirit in the inhabitants of our building and a growing hope in their eyes. They weren't out of the woods yet—but they were on their way. And it was all thanks to Mariah.

The burgeoning romance had added an extra glow to Jasper's eyes. Until now.

My thoughts were distracted by an urgent tug on the wrist to which I had tied one end of the improvised leash. I looked down into a pair of eyes even more anguished than Jasper's. A pleading whimper reinforced the urgency.

'We have to get Tex downstairs,' I said, 'or we won't be responsible for what happens next.'

Another whimper, bordering on a howl, from Tex added weight to my statement. This time Evangeline was allowed to push the lift button without hindrance.

Tex dived into the lift as soon as the doors opened, dragging me with him. Evangeline was able to advance at a more sedate pace. Jasper and Mariah hung back.

'You go ahead,' Jasper said. 'We're in no hurry.'

'You should be.' Mariah tried to push him in. 'That flight is landing in an hour and a half. You don't want to be late.'

Late? Jasper wanted to be missing. It was just as well that Mariah had him in hand; she'd see to it that he met that flight whether he wanted to or not.

'Steady, Tex.' The dog tensed and quivered as the lift doors opened at ground level. I gave my end of the tights another hitch around my wrist and clung on for dear life as he dived for the opening, dragging me across the slippery marble floor.

Behind us, I heard a telephone begin to ring and glanced over my shoulder to see Evangeline burrow into her handbag and retrieve her cellphone. Speaking into it, she followed us at a more leisurely pace, stopping at the top of the long shallow steps to continue her conversation. She did not appear to be enjoying it.

For that matter, I wasn't having such a great time myself. Of all the embarrassing and demeaning human occupations, attending— literally—to a dog's toilet has always ranked high in my perceptions. Now, tethered to a monster hound doing his best to raise the level of the Thames, I was sure of it. He finally finished and looked up at me, wagging his tail

85

expectantly. I realized with horror that he wanted to be taken for a walk to complete the rest of his business.

Where were Lucy and Nova? They were supposed to be here by now to take this beast off our hands. What was keeping them? I looked around frantically.

I saw only Evangeline, descending the steps in a majestic fury, outrage quivering in every fibre of her being. I braced myself.

'What now?' I asked.

'They can't make it.' She glared at Tex as though it was his fault. Perhaps it was. 'And do you know why?'

'How could I? You took the call.' Now that Evangeline was no longer blocking the doorway, there was a flurry of activity up there. Mariah and Jasper emerged cautiously, making sure that Evangeline's attention was distracted and—even better—her back was turned to them. They gave a quick wave and hurried across the pavement and into Mariah's car.

More cautiously still, Nigel moved into the open, hesitating at the top of the steps and looking around carefully. The shadow of the bailiff still hung over him, despite Mariah's best endeavours. It was going to take a lot more time and effort to extricate Nigel from the financial pit he had dug for himself.

He saw us and his face brightened, he came down the steps and headed straight for us. Tex greeted him as an old friend, rearing up to plant his forepaws on Nigel's shoulders and trying to lick his face, uttering ecstatic little yelps.

'Down, Tex!' I tugged at my end of the leash. 'Down!'

'No, no, quite all right.' Nigel stepped back smartly and Tex plopped back to earth. Nigel patted his head. 'Splendid chap, splendid. You must be getting quite attached to him.'

'Only by a length of nylon,' Evangeline said coldly. 'Would you believe it? We've been let down. Nova can't come and take him off our hands as she faithfully promised. Not until tonight. We're stuck with him for the day.'

'Ah!' Nigel brightened still more. I got the feeling that we were playing right into his hands. 'Perhaps I could help. I'd be glad to take him walkies. If you don't mind.'

'Mind!' Tex lurched forward, identifying the magic word 'walkies', nearly throwing me into Nigel's arms. 'We'd be delighted.'

'Ah! Good! So would I.' Nigel exuded satisfaction. 'I have a couple of business meetings. I could bring him along, give him a good outing. If you don't mind my keeping him so long, that is. All afternoon, I'm afraid.'

'Great!' I tried to unwind my end of the tights.

'You can keep him, for all I care,' Evangeline agreed.

'*If* he were ours to give,' I reminded her.

87

'Ah! Just as well, perhaps. No pets allowed, you know.' Nigel eyed my efforts dubiously. He followed the length of nylon leg to the panty bit swaying between Tex and me and looked even more dubious. 'I just want to borrow him for the afternoon. I mean, take him walkies,' he amended hastily.

So that was it. Nigel didn't really care whether poor Tex ever went walkies or not; he had his own agenda. No bailiff or process server was going to come within lunging distance of an enormous dog of unknown disposition. Why should they? They were not paid enough to lay their lives on the line to carry out their lawful pursuits. Nigel would acquire the perfect bodyguard for the price of a brisk walk and perhaps a little embarrassment.

'Er, thank you.' He accepted the foot of my half of the tights, the other foot was firmly tied to Tex's collar. The panty part waved like a flag in the breeze. He winced as he looked at it.

'Well, I'm sorry, but it was all I had,' I explained. Evangeline snorted.

'Oh, quite. Quite. Quite all right.' He winced again. 'Perhaps we might find something more suitable along the way.'

'Let me contribute to the cost.' I knew Nigel had very little money; I tried not to think how little. Evangeline snorted again as I took a twenty-pound note from my bag and gave it to Nigel; he could buy a leash and have enough left over for a good meal at least.

'Ah! Well! If you insist—'

'I do,' I said firmly.

'Ah! I'm sure we can find something for that. Perhaps even some change—'

'Never mind that,' I said, even more firmly. 'Just take Tex away and give him a good run—'

'For the money,' Evangeline finished. 'And you needn't bother to bring him back.'

'You'd better,' I said. 'We've got to return him to his owner.'

'Why?' Evangeline asked.

'Ah! Quite! Quite!' Nigel began backing away. He wasn't going to get involved in any arguments.

Tex suddenly realized that events were moving onwards and the promised walkies was going to happen. He gathered himself and sprinted forward, dragging Nigel in his wake. Sooner him than me. I hoped the tights held together long enough for Nigel to reach a pet store. It was cheap at the price.

'There,' Evangeline said with satisfaction as they receded into the distance. 'That's one problem disposed of.' Ominously, she added, 'We'll deal with the other this evening.'

'What other?' I didn't really want to know, but it had to be asked.

'Nova and Lucy.' She flared her nostrils dramatically. 'And their treachery.'

'Treachery?' I echoed weakly.

'Treachery!' she snarled. 'Do you know why they aren't here this morning?' Fortunately, she didn't wait for an answer. 'Because they're having lunch with Sweetums Carew! Sweetums went to the show Lucy is assistant stage-managing at the Emperor Uncloth'd. She talked to Lucy about the script Lucy is working on now.'

'Uh-oh!'

'Uh-oh, indeed! They are going to discuss it further over lunch.' Evangeline narrowed her eyes. 'I will not have another script stolen out from under me!'

'The script might not be any good,' I suggested tentatively, remembering her narrow escape with the abysmal *Queen Leah.*

'Nonsense!' Evangeline had never agreed with my assessment of that script. Well, she wouldn't, would she? Not when it was such a plum leading role for her. 'Lucy is a brilliant playwright. Any moment now the world will recognize her genius.'

'Uh-huh.'

'I've told Nova not to let Lucy sign anything. We're going to the Emperor Uncloth'd ourselves tonight.'

'Are we?' This was news to me, I'd been hoping for a quiet evening at home. We were overdue for one.

'We'll turn Tex over to them there and they can return him tomorrow. More importantly, we'll find out what Lucy is working on.'

'Uh-huh.' I didn't think I was strong enough for that. Not now. Maybe never. 'Meanwhile, how about something to eat?'

'Yes, yes.' But her impatience was not entirely genuine. I heard her stomach rumble faintly.

'Get your cellphone out and see if you can whistle up Eddie and his cab,' I said. 'He can take us to the supermarket. That hound has just about eaten us out of house and home.'

CHAPTER EIGHT

True to her word ('For a change,' Evangeline grumbled), Nova collected us at about seven that evening. We all piled into the cab, Tex settling down on the floor of the back seat with a contented sigh, and headed off into the unknown.

Unknown to us. Nova drove with expert precision along narrow streets, cutting down dark byways and barely lit passages that had never been designed for motor cars or even horse-drawn carriages. We were deep in *terra incognita* when she rounded a final corner and drew up in front of a low dark building crouching in a murky alleyway. A heavy mist was rolling in from somewhere to the rear of the building.

Thump-thump-thump. One of us was happy, at least.

'This is it? We're here?' I hoped Nova would

91

say something like, 'No, we've just run out of petrol' or, 'We have a flat tyre', but she got out of the cab and came round to open the door with a flourish.

'The Emperor Uncloth'd,' she announced. 'Isn't that a great pub sign?'

We looked upward as she gestured. It might have been an illustration from the Hans Christian Andersen fairy tales. A plump complacent gentleman wearing a crown, with orb and sceptre discreetly positioned, followed by a smirking page boy holding an invisible train clear of the ground, pranced down a street between lines of goggling peasants.

I made a mental bet that the locals had some very interesting nicknames for this particular pub.

Tex bounded out of the cab and stood waiting for us, tail wagging, looking around with interest. This was his kind of territory. He could hardly wait to see what would happen next.

I was surveying the scene without any such anticipation. The lights glowing within the pub were too dim to be welcoming. They must have paid their electricity bill, I told myself, otherwise they wouldn't have any lights at all. Perhaps there was one of those power cuts in force where they lowered the power rather than cutting it off completely.

'Are we near the river?' There was an increasingly heavy damp mist, if not downright fog, curling along the narrow passage.

'The canal,' Nova said. 'We're miles away from the river here. Miles away from anywhere, really,' she added wistfully. 'That's why they've started running this theatre. They're hoping to pull in more customers with it.'

'Uh-huh.' I gazed at the poster displayed in the window. I didn't think they were going to attract a lot of custom with this offering: 'THE CRUMBL'D WALL, a Modern Tragedy in Blank Verse'. Not unless they had a disproportionate number of masochists in the catchment area.

'Come along, Trixie.' Evangeline glanced at the poster and barely quailed. 'You want to see Lucy again, don't you?'

Actually, I didn't. I could live out the rest of my life quite happily if I never saw Lucy again. And that went for Nova, too.

Evangeline didn't wait for a reply. She pushed open the saloon bar door and entered. Tex shoved ahead of me, panting and eager, the smells obviously familiar and home-like to him. I wondered if he'd be disappointed not to discover any of his old friends inside. So far, he hadn't seemed to be missing anyone, not even his master.

'Do you see what I see?' Evangeline halted in mid-stride and stiffened. I stopped just in time to keep from bumping into her and followed her gaze.

'Hello, Sweetums,' I said. Well, someone

had to say something. Evangeline was just standing there glaring at her. The same young man was at her side; I tried to remember his name.

'Evangeline Sinclair and Trixie Dolan!' He had no such trouble with ours. 'We meet again!' Sweetums gave him a nasty look; he didn't have to sound so enthusiastic about it.

'Hello, girls.' She widened her eyes. 'What are you doing here?'

'Nova and Lucy have been dear friends for ages.' Evangeline wasted no time in firing a warning shot across Sweetums's bow. 'In fact, I nearly starred in Lucy's last play.'

'How interesting.' Sweetums lost no time in returning fire. '*I'm* starring in her *next* play.'

They faced each other like two dogs growling over a coveted bone that lay between them. Perhaps that wasn't very complimentary to Lucy—or perhaps it was. An untried playwright with two major actresses warring over her next, still unfinished, play, had to be flattered by such a situation. It was enough to go to anyone's head.

Out of the corner of my eye, I saw Nova start towards us, then halt as she took in the situation and decided she didn't want to get involved until it had cooled a bit. She veered off and headed in the opposite direction, towards a doorway outlined in very low-wattage lightbulbs which had to lead to the performance area. Tex loped after her.

'Let me get you two a drink.' Sweetums's escort could not possibly be as oblivious to every undercurrent as he appeared. Could he?

'A large brandy.' Evangeline glanced at the poster displayed on the bar and shuddered. 'An extra large one,' she amended, obviously remembering the usual size of British measures.

'Sounds good to me,' I seconded.

'And I'll have a refill, Terence, dear.' Sweetums underlined her proprietary rights.

'Right you are.' Terence pulled out a billfold, the bulk of which allayed any misgivings I might have had about the expense of our order. Not that I had many; any male squiring Sweetums around had to have plenty in his pocket and more in reserve.

A man in the centre of a group of young men at the other end of the bar raised his glass to us. Then one of the other men did, then another. We were recognized.

The trouble was that some of them looked familiar to me. To tell the truth, most of them did. I realized that they must be regulars on the pub theatre circuit and were saluting us, not only for our past achievements, but as new recruits to their ranks.

Evangeline inclined her head graciously and gave them a wave in lieu of raising the glass she had not yet acquired. I did the same, albeit with a vague feeling of apprehension. We were opening the gates to who knew what

95

barbarians might be lurking without.

Sweetums pouted prettily and not only raised her glass, but fluttered her fingers, too. In another couple of seconds, she was going to invite them to join us and to peel her a grape.

Fortunately, Terence returned with our drinks just then and, simultaneously, the bell rang to signal that the performance was about to start. We picked up our drinks and followed the crowd.

I might have known it. Beyond the lighted doorway, a long narrow flight of stairs twisted upwards. Couldn't any of these people produce a play on the ground floor? We both halted at the foot of the stairs and looked at them gloomily.

'Need any help?' An arm was offered—not Terence's, luckily, or Sweetums would have torn it off and beaten him over the head with it.

'I can manage quite well, thank you!' Evangeline snapped. 'I'm simply wondering whether it will be worth the effort.'

'Oh, certainly. Sorry.' He snatched his arm back as though fearing she might bite it.

'We've met before, haven't we?' Perhaps that was putting it a bit too strongly, but I wanted to cool the situation. 'Now where—?'

'At *The Lower Depths*,' he said eagerly. 'At the Red Bull. I'm Vic Varney.'

'Of course you are,' I said warmly, ignoring Evangeline's snort. It might have been an inane remark, but at least it was polite—which was

96

more than Evangeline could manage.

'Come along, Trixie, you're blocking the way.' Evangeline turned and ascended the stairs at a pace that could do her no good.

I looked around. True, a few people had piled up behind Vic, but most of the audience were sidestepping us without trouble and heading up the stairs. The young men hovering behind Vic were the ones he had been drinking with in the corner and it was only too obvious from their hopeful expressions that they were far more interested in meeting us than in rushing upstairs to the performance.

Sweetums caught the prevailing mood, too. She beamed at the massed faces. An audience was an audience. 'Why, Vic,' she said, 'aren't you going to introduce us to your friends?'

'What?' He had been gazing after Evangeline with the look of a hunting dog who had just seen a plump juicy pigeon get away. 'What? Oh, yes, of course. Sorry.' He shuffled uneasily, as though pushed from behind, and glanced over his shoulder at the expectant faces.

'Adam, Mark, Paul, Greg and Ledbetter.' He reeled off the names while their owners acknowledged them with a wave.

'Ledbetter?' Sweetums arched her eyebrows, unaware that the use of a surname often denoted a more intimate acquaintanceship than the use of a first name. 'What an unusual name.'

'Unusual person,' someone said from the back and raised a laugh from the others.

'Ledbetter is a very unusual person,' Vic said earnestly, lest we get the wrong idea. 'He's the stake-holder.'

Someone murmured in protest behind him and his face flushed a deep red. Somehow, he had put his foot in it.

'I mean—' he began.

'If he's got a stake, he must be after you girls.' Sweetums saw her cue and pounced on it, her laugh tinkling out merrily. 'They've just finished that Dracula picture,' she explained to the others, who were looking uneasy. 'They must be used to stakes by now. And silver bullets, too.'

Aha! I hadn't realized it had rankled so much with Sweetums that we had a new film coming out soon. Dracula or not, a job was a job—and it was a long time since Sweetums had graced the Silver Screen.

'Oh, no, it's not that sort of stake.' Vic blushed even deeper. 'It's stake, as in betting—'

A low warning growl behind him coincided with the clang of the final warning bell.

'I mean,' he said hastily. 'We have the occasional flutter among ourselves. A pool on the Derby, or who'll make the highest individual score in the darts tournament, that sort of thing.' His brow was beaded with perspiration, he looked over his shoulder to his friends for their approval.

'Trix-ieee...' Evangeline called from the top of the stairs. 'Hurry along, you're holding up the show.'

'We're coming.' Sweetums moved forward and clutched at Terence's arm. 'Oooh, why are your stairs always so steep and uneven?'

'Old building,' Terence said. 'Mind that step. Most of them were dwelling places originally. The staircases were deliberately constructed with one or two steps higher than the others. The householders knew which ones they were; the theory was that any thief sneaking in during the night would stumble on the uneven step and rouse the house or, with any luck, fall and break a leg or perhaps kill himself. Life was cheap in those days—especially for the criminal element.'

Someone sniggered behind us and it occurred to me that it wasn't particularly tactful of Terence to speak so disparagingly of the criminal element in this neighbourhood. It might even be dangerous.

'Oh, isn't he wonderful?' Sweetums cried. 'He knows everything! You just have to ask him a question and you've got the answer.'

I recognized the sound of Evangeline grinding her teeth again as I drew abreast of her.

'There do not appear to be any seats available,' she announced grimly.

'Plenty of seats.' Vic looked around. 'Move

99

along there, you chaps,' he directed.

I saw, with sinking heart, that it was amphitheatre seating: padded benches with no divisions between the seats. Seats? They were nothing but spaces—and no back to them, either, just the rise of the next tier of benching so that, if you leaned back incautiously, you risked getting the toes of someone's shoe in the back of your neck.

Terence had bustled Sweetums to the end of one of the rows and was busy clearing a place for them in the centre of the row.

'No, oh, no, thank you,' I said as someone stood to allow us to get past. 'I'll just sit here at the end, thank you.' Near the exit. I knew which side my bread was buttered on.

'Yes, that will do.' Evangeline gave me a push and sat down on the very end space, ensuring that *she* was not cheek by jowl with any of the groundlings.

I glanced sideways at the man I was inadvertently snuggling up next to and was not reassured by what I saw. How pleased I'll be when the vogue for designer stubble has run its course. The audience beyond him did not look any more prepossessing. They were probably all quite respectable students, and possibly lecturers, at the London School of Economics but, in the half-light, they managed to look amazingly sinister.

The clearing at the bottom of the tiers of benches—I wouldn't dignify it by calling it a stage—provided no reassurance, either, although the crumbling pile of masonry in the centre of it had something familiar about it. Could it be meant to be the Berlin Wall? Were they writing would-be epics about that already?

'You'll be happy to know there *is* an interval in this one,' a voice said behind me. I turned as much as I was able and saw one of the young men from downstairs. Combining that remark with the piercing blue eyes gazing at me intently, I was now able to identify him as the man who had been behind me in the audience at *Farewell, Everyone.*

'Oh, thank you ... er, Adam?' I smiled at him and he nodded. 'That *is* comforting to know.'

'Thought it would cheer you. How are you feeling now?'

'Feeling? Oh, just fi—' In the nick of time, Evangeline nudged me, reminding me not to give away our escape plan.

'Oh, better, thank you,' I amended quickly. 'Although it *is* rather close in here, isn't it?'

'Not a breath of air,' he acknowledged cheerfully. 'But it's better than it was before they banned smoking.'

There was a flurry of activity in what passed for the wings and I heard a friendly 'Woof'. Then we were plunged into Stygian darkness for long enough for me to note with foreboding that there was no dimly glowing EXIT sign over

101

the doorway. Did that mean there was no emergency lighting? And wasn't that against fire regulations?

Distracted by that and by the rustlings and stumblings as the actors assumed their places, I was barely aware that someone had knelt beside Evangeline and was whispering a message to her.

It was really quite peaceful there in the darkness, then they went and spoiled it. A baby spot appeared out of nowhere and centred on an anguished mask of a face. The performance had begun.

* * *

I had fully intended to nurse my drink along so that it lasted until the interval, but the worse the play got, the faster I sipped. I was simply not attuned to blank verse. Was it possible that pub landlords deliberately chose the worst plays available because they made people drink faster? Talk about popcorn sales keeping the cinemas going in lean times! When the interval finally arrived, I had been clutching an empty glass for what seemed like hours, if not years.

Sweetums was already on her feet and trampling toes in her dash for the exit. Yelps of pain and hisses of rage marked her progress. Terence followed more slowly, apologizing profusely all the way and trying to smooth the ruffled feelings she left in her wake.

'Coming downstairs for a drink!' It was an order as much as a question. Sweetums paused beside our row, tapping one foot impatiently.

'Yes, good idea.' The response was so unlike Evangeline that I glanced at her in surprise, just in time to spot the twitch of her fingers as she undid the catch of her handbag and stood up awkwardly. The handbag fell to the floor, gaping open and spilling its contents down the steps.

'Oh, dear!' Evangeline watched a lipstick roll down the steps and across the stage. 'How clumsy of me.'

'Yes.' Sweetums compressed her lips and stared at the debris at Evangeline's feet as I bent to start picking up items. 'We'll see you downstairs,' Sweetums said, making it clear that she wasn't going to help clear up.

I kept my head down as Terence came up to us and stooped to retrieve a small vial of perfume.

'Come along, Terence,' Sweetums ordered imperiously. 'The girls will follow when they've sorted themselves out.' She made it sound unlikely that we ever would.

Adam had trotted to the foot of the steps and was groping under a chunk of concrete for the lipstick.

'Are you all right?' Vic made a move towards uncapping the small flask of smelling salts he had picked up.

'Quite all right, thank you.' Evangeline took the flask and replaced it in her handbag. 'You go ahead—' She waved the others onwards. 'I think we'll just stay here for the interval.'

'If you're sure?' Vic looked around, but the floor was clear now. 'Perhaps we could bring you back a drink?' Some of the others had already started ahead.

'No, no, we're—'

There was a scuffle and a shriek, followed by several shouts and cries from the staircase. Evangeline looked towards it hopefully.

'What's going on here?' Vic abandoned us and raced for the stairs. 'Is everything all right?'

'Perfectly all right. Don't worry,' Sweetums trilled. 'My darling Terence wouldn't let me fall.'

'Not until he knows her better,' Evangeline muttered.

CHAPTER NINE

'Come on.' Evangeline stuffed everything back into her handbag carelessly and stood up. 'We're going backstage to see Lucy.'

The auditorium had emptied and Nova had appeared at the edge of the performance area and was beckoning to us urgently.

'Hurry up before Sweetums begins to

suspect anything.' Evangeline started forward. 'We want to talk to Lucy by ourselves.'

'We do?' But she was way ahead of me now. I sighed and followed her.

'Lucy has her own office,' Nova said proudly, leading us to the smallest room I had ever seen without white porcelain fittings in it. When we were all inside, we had to inhale and squeeze together before Nova could shut the door. It didn't help that Tex was sprawled across most of the floor space; his tail thumped a greeting to us.

'All that's missing is the Marx Brothers,' I muttered. To myself, of course, nobody else was paying any attention. Evangeline and Lucy were air-kissing an enthusiastic greeting.

'*Dear* Lucy, it seems such ages!' Evangeline stepped back, Tex whimpered and moved his paw hastily. 'Let me look at you. How well you look! Doesn't she look well, Trixie?'

'Great.' Anything would have been an improvement, but Lucy did seem to be looking a bit less harassed, also as though she'd had a few regular meals. Steady employment, such as it was, seemed to agree with her.

'Tell her about your new play, Lu.' Nova obviously felt the preliminaries had gone on long enough. 'She's just dying to hear all about it.'

'Yes, indeed,' Evangeline cooed. 'Nova has been whetting my appetite.'

'Well, I don't know.' Lucy glanced at Nova

105

uneasily. 'We've more than half promised it to Sweetums Carew.'

'Oh, well, in that case, we wouldn't want you to break your word,' I said quickly. It was worth a try.

'Sweetums Carew!' Evangeline drew herself up, attempting to annihilate me with a passing glance, but concentrating the main force of her energy on Lucy. 'Are you suggesting that Sweetums Carew could *ever* play a role that would be suitable for *me?*'

'Oh, no. No.' Lucy quailed visibly. 'She'd give a completely different interpretation of the role. It would be another play, almost.'

'There's no *almost* about it,' Evangeline said severely. 'It would cease to be the play you had in mind and turn into a *vehicle* for Sweetums. She'll simper and toss her head—' Evangeline demonstrated grotesquely. 'She'll roll her eyes, she may even lisp in the more emotional moments—'

'Oh, stop!' Lucy covered her face with her hands. 'Stop!'

'You'd lose all control over your play,' Evangeline continued relentlessly. 'Is that what you want?'

'You *did* have Evangeline in mind for the part,' Nova said reproachfully. 'From the moment you first got the idea.'

'I know. I know—and she'd be magnificent in the role.' Lucy lowered her hands to gaze tragically at Nova. 'But she disappeared and

106

we didn't know where to find her. And then Terence brought Sweetums Carew along and she was *so* persuasive.'

Off in the distance, a warning bell sounded for the start of the second act.

'How much?' Evangeline demanded grimly. 'How much did she offer to steal *my* play?'

'Excuse me,' I broke in quickly before Evangeline got carried away and started raising the ante. 'But shouldn't we know a bit more about this play before we get too excited? I mean, it hasn't even been written yet, has it?'

'I have the first ten pages done,' Lucy said.

'And it's brilliant,' Nova said enthusiastically. 'The best thing you've ever done, Lu. Wait till it hits the stage—it will sweep the boards. It's a dead cert for the *Evening Standard* Award. And, when it hits New York, the Tony, the Emmy, the Critics' Circle—'

'Uh-huh.' I'd prefer to hear rave reviews from somebody other than the playwright's best friend. 'But what makes it so great? What is it about?'

'Yes.' Rather belatedly, Evangeline accepted that a note of caution might be in order, but an acquisitive gleam still lurked at the back of her eyes. 'What is it about?'

'Wait till you hear it,' Nova said. 'The title alone will get you. Hit 'em with it, Lu.'

'Yes.' Lucy drew herself up proudly and announced: '*Hamlet Swoons.*'

107

'*Hamlet*...?' I echoed faintly. '*Swoons*...?' I wondered if I was going to swoon myself.

The second warning bell sounded.

'Well, it's not exactly *Hamlet* Hamlet,' Lucy said. 'Not as such.'

'It isn't?' I braced myself.

'Actually—' Lucy looked over her shoulder, as though rival playwrights might be waiting to steal the idea. 'Actually, it's Sarah Bernhardt playing Hamlet. She did, you know. And after a great success with it in Paris, she brought the show to London in 1899. It was a very controversial production.'

'I'll bet it was,' I muttered.

'Two Parisian critics fought a duel over it,' Nova said proudly. 'That will come into it, too. It isn't just a straight *Hamlet*.'

'I'm sure it isn't.' Straight was never a word I had associated with Lucy and Nova. 'Was this before or after she lost her leg?'

'Before,' Lucy said. 'It was *L'Aiglon* she continued appearing in afterwards—and did it very well, too.'

'The theatre is all about illusion, after all.' Evangeline was rapt. In her case, read 'delusion' along with 'illusion'.

'And the Prince of Wales was one of Bernhardt's lovers,' Nova added enticingly.

'Playing Bernhardt playing Hamlet...' Evangeline's eyes glazed over. '"To be or not to be"...' she murmured throatily and I knew she was hooked.

The awful thing was, I could see it wasn't a bad idea. OK, maybe even a good idea, bordering on the great. It would all depend on the execution—and that was the operative word. Could Lucy be trusted not to kill it stone dead? But it was Lucy's idea and she had to be given the chance to work it out. Oh, yes, and there was one other fly in the ointment.

'That's all right for you,' I said to Evangeline. 'But where do I come in? We were going to do a play together, remember?'

'Yes, yes.' Evangeline waved a hand airily. 'I'm sure there'll be something for you to do. Bernhardt must have travelled with a maid.'

'Now see here, Evangeline Sinclair, I haven't reached this age and stage in my career to go back to playing French maids!'

'You needn't worry about that!' A new voice burst into the conversation. We all jumped and looked towards the door, where Sweetums Carew stood seething. 'That play is mine! You have nothing to do with it—or in it!'

Damn! With Evangeline, you knew where you were—she stamped around, never missing an opportunity to leap into a good rousing scene. But Sweetums was sly; she sneaked around, listening outside, opening doors silently. You never knew she was there until it was too late.

'*You* could never play this part!' Evangeline whirled, eyes flashing fire, to face this invader.

The final bell sounded. Tex growled softly.

109

'Sweetums ... Miss Carew ... Sweetums...' a voice bleated behind her. 'The second act ... we ought to get back to our seats.' A miserable Terence, completely out of his depth, reached out a hand to touch her shoulder, wisely thought better of it and withdrew it. 'The show is starting again.'

Wrong. Maybe the show was starting, but all the action was going on right here.

'And you!' Sweetums ignored Evangeline and turned her fury on Lucy. 'You *promised* that play to *me!* I *paid* you for it! That play is mine! Try giving it to anyone else and you'll regret it for the rest of your life!'

Which might not be very long. I could fill in the blank as well as the next one. Especially when the next one didn't know Sweetums so well.

'Sweetums...' Terence pleaded. Behind him, I could see the actors hurrying past to take their places. 'Sweetums ... please. Everyone will be waiting for us to take our seats.'

'Of course they will.' Abruptly, Sweetums reverted to typecasting and sent a radiant smile over her shoulder to Terence. He still looked nervous, as well he might.

'Just remember'—she dropped the mask, turning back to glare at Evangeline—'that play is *mine*. You'll never have it!'

The door slammed behind her. Tex growled again.

'Oh, dear.' Lucy stared at the door, wringing

110

her hands. 'Do you think she's terribly upset?'

'Just don't open any surprise gifts,' I said.

'Lucy,' Nova said. '*Did* you take any money from her?'

'It was two hundred pounds,' Lucy said miserably. 'And the rent was due.'

'Oh, Lucy!' Nova slumped against the wall.

'Did you *sign* anything?' Evangeline went straight to the heart of the matter.

'I don't think so,' Lucy said uncertainly. 'Nothing like a contract. There was just some kind of a receipt, but there was no writing on it.'

'A blank cheque!' Evangeline joined Nova against the wall. 'Sweetums could write anything she wanted in the empty space.'

'Look—' I tried to shift the situation into some sort of reality. 'Shouldn't we have a sight of what all the fuss is about? Those ten pages you've already written, Lucy—how about letting us see them?'

'Oh, I don't know about that.' Lucy's chin thrust forward in an unexpected stubbornness. 'It's all at such a delicate stage right now. I can't bear to let anyone see it, to have anyone else's thoughts or reactions impinging on my subconscious.'

Over her head, Nova met my eyes and gave me the nod. We would see those ten pages.

'Oh! But we're keeping you from the performance!' Lucy looked stricken and tried a diversionary tactic. 'You must get back to your

111

seats. The last act is starting.'

'Mmmm...' Evangeline passed a hand over her forehead, her eyes closing and an expression of great suffering nobly borne appearing on her face. 'I think not. My head. I'm sorry. Please make my excuses, but I must go home and lie down.'

'She's understating the agony, she always does.' I picked up my cue and moved to her side—she wasn't going to escape and leave me here. 'I'll see her back to the flat. I know what it's like when she has one of her heads. I'm afraid the evening is over. If someone could call us a taxi ...?'

'I'll drive you,' Nova said. 'I'll come back for you later, Lu.'

Tex heaved himself to his feet at these signs of activity. He looked from us to Lucy, hesitating. Lucy met his eyes and dropped a hand to tangle in his ruff, tugging it gently. An expression of deep affection passed between them.

'We'll drop the dog off at the Green Colleen on our way home,' Nova assured us. 'You don't have to worry about a thing.'

'Except what we're going to do next.' Evangeline was bound to mount some kind of campaign against Sweetums.

'Tomorrow is Sunday.' Evangeline frowned at me meaningfully. 'A day of rest. And we are going to rest.'

Famous last words.

112

*　　　*　　　*

At least we got to sleep in fairly late. For this relief, much thanks. Then raised voices began to ring through my dreams, disturbing me and bringing that restless pre-waking consciousness.

Then the doorbell pealed and went on pealing, an endless, relentless, insistent demand that brooked no disobedience. I struggled into my dressing gown and almost collided with Evangeline, still tying the ends of her own sash as we stumbled towards the door. Anything to stop that incessant racket.

'All right! All right!' Evangeline snarled. 'We're coming!'

The bell continued to peal, even after we had flung open the door and stepped back to allow Beauregard Sylvester to enter. For an anxious moment, I wondered whether Jasper had collapsed against the bell button and was ringing out his last moments. Probably it just felt like that to him. His grandfather's face was a thundercloud of unforgiving fury; Beau looked neither left nor right as he stormed into the living room, coming to rest at last in front of the red plush sofa—obviously the first item he recognized in the entire flat.

Evangeline wheeled and followed in Beau's wake, but I waited until Jasper had pulled himself away from the button and, supported by Mariah, stumbled unseeingly after them.

A tall elegant woman with an enigmatic but striking face walked slowly behind Jasper. She glanced in my direction and her lips twitched in a mirthless smile. She acted almost as though she knew me, but I had never seen her before in my life.

'Jasper ... Come on, Jasper.' Mariah prodded him tentatively, impelling him forward. 'Straight ahead. That's right. You can do it...'

He stumbled into the entrance hall. Both women sailed in majestically behind him.

'What the hell is going on here?' Beau bellowed. 'I turn my back for a few weeks and everything goes to pieces.' He did not sound entirely dissatisfied with the thought. Who wants to come back from a trip and find out that the world has been getting along perfectly well without them?

Before closing the door, I took another look around the outer foyer. Where was Juanita? And who was this strange woman with Beau? Had he finally replaced Juanita with a younger model and, if so, were we about to be informed? Or was he just going to let us guess it for ourselves?

'I recognize the sofa.' Beau stared hard at the piece of furniture, as though he half expected it to disappear in a puff of smoke.

'The chaise longue is over there,' Jasper pointed out. 'And the armchairs. All the

114

furniture is here—it's just . . . spread out more.'

'You saved the furniture,' Beau said sarcastically. 'Ain't that just great? It was the *house* that was worth the real money, you idiot!'

Jasper knew that, of course. That was why it was the house he had mortgaged. Who'd bother lending him money on the furniture? He flinched and ducked, as though in expectation of a blow.

Even Mariah looked at him impatiently. He had obviously lost a certain amount of ground with her since the arrival of his grandfather.

'Sit down and have a drink, Beau,' Evangeline said. She flashed a signal to me and we both started for the kitchen.

'Who is that woman?' Evangeline spoke as soon as we were out of earshot of the others. 'What has he done with Juanita?'

Beau's voice rose in the distance, hectoring his unfortunate grandson.

'Your guess is as good as mine.' I jumped at the sound of a fist hitting a table. 'You haven't read anything about a passenger being lost at sea, have you?'

'He wouldn't dare!' Evangeline glanced nervously towards the living room. 'Would he?'

'Wouldn't he?' We met each other's eyes in dark surmise. Death was cheaper than divorce—and Beau was the tightwad of all time.

115

'That boy will be the ruination of me!' Beau stormed into the kitchen and stood there glaring at us as though it were our fault. 'That beautiful house in St John's Wood is gone and this half-finished dump is in negative equity. Thank God I never underwrote any of his so-called investments. That boy can spend money faster than any normal human being can make it!'

Evangeline generated an inordinate amount of noise tumbling ice cubes from the refrigerator trays into the ice bucket.

'Here.' She thrust the ice bucket at Beau. 'Take this into the living room and sit down and have a drink and calm down.'

'Have you two taken to drinking at this hour of the morning?' Ungrateful, he looked down at the ice bucket disapprovingly.

'It's not morning,' I said. 'It's half past noon.'

'That late already?' Beau shook his head. 'Where did the morning get to?'

'Doesn't time go fast when you're having fun?' Evangeline murmured. So she, too, had been awakened by the raised voices from the penthouse across the hall. Probably everybody on the floor below had been disturbed, too. Beau had a fine carrying voice and Jasper's anguished bleat wasn't so far behind.

I went straight to the drinks trolley in the corner of the living room and began pouring drinks. It was a good hostess-like occupation and it kept me out of firing range.

'Let me help.' Mariah came over and began ferrying drinks to the guests. She was looking pale and shaken; she'd spent yesterday and this morning in the midst of the hostilities. You had to give her full marks for staying power.

Beau accepted his drink and retreated to stand at the floor-to-ceiling window with his back to the room, brooding out over the impressive riverscape.

'It's a magnificent view.' For once, Evangeline tried to pour oil on the troubled waters.

'I've seen better.' He took a deep swallow.

'I'm sure.' Evangeline took a deep swallow herself and persevered. 'You must tell us all about your trip.'

'It was too damned expensive!' If she had been trying to raise his spirits, she had failed.

'I thought you'd come back a lot sooner than you planned.' Somehow, Evangeline's good intentions never last long; malice was creeping back into her voice.

I turned to look at the others and felt a faint sense of revulsion. It was disgusting the way Jasper was cosying-up to his grandfather's new lady. Did he hope to curry favour with Beau that way? Or was he hoping that he could enlist the woman on his side?

The latter seemed a more realistic proposition, judging from the way the woman was responding to his attentions. She nodded

117

encouragingly as he spoke to her earnestly, then stretched out a hand to brush a lock of hair back from his forehead.

Wait a minute!! That was moving pretty fast for a newly introduced stranger who was usurping his grandmother's place.

I tilted my head and half closed my eyes to get the proper out-of-perspective view. That blurred the woman's face and, without that distraction, her form began to appear more familiar. Just then she dropped a quick comforting kiss on her grandson's ashen face and began patting his hand consolingly.

'Good Lord—Juanita!' I gasped. 'I didn't recognize you!'

'The plastic surgeon was too damned expensive, too,' Beau grumbled. 'Cost a fortune.'

'You've *got* a fortune,' Juanita said coldly.

'I won't have, the way you're carrying on. Between you and that grandson of yours—'

'*Ours.*'

'Whatever.' Beau shrugged and tossed down the rest of his drink. 'Y'all keep on like this and I'm gonna be bankrupt, that's all I know.'

'Poor boy,' Juanita purred. 'He is down to his last five million.'

'It's not that much!' Beau yelped indignantly. 'Nowhere near that much. I keep telling you.'

'It is more like ten, I think.' Juanita was still purring. She was a woman who could

118

recognize the upper hand when she held it.

'Nothing like it! You're crazy! You're trying to ruin me!' Beau raised his glass to his lips with a gesture that should have tossed the contents down his throat. He choked on air and looked at the empty glass incredulously. 'What does a man have to do to get a refill around here?'

Mariah darted forward to take his glass and bring it to me. I recklessly splashed a large quantity of Scotch into it. Juanita watched with disapproval. I waited for her to make some comment, but she didn't. A frown that scarcely rippled her newly smooth face followed Mariah as she brought the glass to Beau.

'Anyone else?' I called out merrily, hoping to avert the outright quarrel that seemed to be threatening.

'It is time to eat, I think.' Juanita turned to Jasper. 'You spoke of reservations?'

'Downstairs,' Jasper said. 'Sophie and Frederick serve Sunday lunch. It goes on all afternoon and you'll get to meet some of the other residents.'

'You think that's an inducement?' Half of Beau's drink disappeared abruptly. 'Anybody would have to be crazy to live here. Why should we want to meet them?'

'The food is wonderful,' Mariah chimed in on a more practical note. 'Gourmet cooking. Delicious.'

'Well...' Against his better judgement, Beau

was going to allow himself to be persuaded. 'I *am* kinda hungry.' He looked at Evangeline and me. 'You two coming along?'

'It's begun raining—pouring.' Mariah had an air of desperation. She didn't want to be trapped into an intimate meal with Jasper and his terrifying grandparents. 'You'll never find a taxi.'

'We've already made reservations,' I admitted. 'We'll get dressed and meet you downstairs.'

'And'—Evangeline made a grand gesture—'I will even look at your holiday snapshots over lunch.'

'We don't have snapshots,' Beau growled. 'We just have shopping receipts.'

CHAPTER TEN

We got back to our apartment later than we had expected. After a long and leisurely lunch, Jasper and Mariah had managed to make their getaway, while Evangeline and I had gone back to their borrowed penthouse with Beau and Juanita, who could be very good company once Beau's grievances had been aired.

'I'll get it.' The telephone was ringing as we entered and I went ahead while Evangeline switched on the light.

'Hello?' A strange gurgling sound seemed to

be coming from the other end of the line. 'Hello?'

'Aaargh!' A furious male voice snarled out: 'In any right-thinking country, they *hang* people like you!'

'I beg your pardon? What number are you calling?' There was a crashing noise in my ear. 'Hello? Hello?'

'What is it?' Evangeline came into the room.

'Wrong number. I hope.' I replaced the receiver. 'Some very irate man just informed me that they hang people like me in right-thinking countries.'

'The world is full of critics,' Evangeline said. 'Obviously, someone just caught up with one of your old films.'

'Very funny. You don't suppose it has anything to do with Sweetums, do you?'

'Did it sound like Terence?' Evangeline dropped into an armchair, kicked off her shoes and stretched luxuriously, not even bothering to stifle a yawn.

'No. I can't imagine Terence getting that passionate about anything. It was a different kind of voice, rougher and...' the yawn was catching; I gave way to one of my own.

'Since the implication seems to be that this *isn't* a right-thinking country,' Evangeline said, 'I suggest you stop worrying about it and go to bed. It's been a long day.'

'It's always a long day when Beau is around.' But she was right. We were safe in our castle

121

with the drawbridge up. No one could get at us and it was probably a wrong number anyway.

'I'll think about it tomorrow,' I said.

* * *

About three o'clock the next afternoon, I discovered why we had been having such a quiet day: Evangeline had unplugged the telephone.

'There!' Beau reeled in the limp cord and dangled the useless connection in the air. 'No wonder I couldn't get through to you.'

'How long have you been trying?' Evangeline took the wind out of his sails.

'Well...' He deflated visibly. 'The past half-hour at least. Juanita said you'd never be out on a day like this.'

'Oh, did she?' Evangeline tried to look as though she went for an hour's jog through wind and rain and sleet and gloom of night every day of her life. 'What does she know about our habits?'

'Nothing good!' Beau guffawed. 'Walked right into that one, didn't you?'

Anyway, he was in a good mood. With a dirty look at Evangeline, I removed the cord from his hand and plugged the jack into the socket.

'Juanita wants to know what she should wear tonight.' Beau got down to business. 'The Versace gold lamé or the Lacroix black lace?'

122

'The Marks and Spencer jacket and skirt is more the order of dress,' Evangeline said.

'After all I paid for those designer rags? That can't be right. It's Opening Night!' We had invited Beau and Juanita to join us for the new show at the Happy Larry, since it promised to be cheerful.

'Face it, Beau,' Evangeline sighed. 'People don't dress up for Opening Nights in the West End any more—and this is just a pub theatre. The world isn't what it used to be.'

The telephone rang and I picked up the receiver automatically. 'Hello?'

'Who am I talking to?' An arrogant male voice demanded.

'If you don't know, why did you dial my number?' I wasn't going to be caught that way.

'Aaargh! I know you now,' the voice ranted. 'And I've reconsidered. Hanging's too good for you, you dirty—'

I yanked the jack out of the socket.

'Another wrong number?' Evangeline inquired sweetly.

'There's a lot of them around.'

'Maybe you ought to change your number, if you're having trouble,' Beau suggested.

'Maybe we ought,' I agreed absently, still holding the echo of that hostile voice. It definitely wasn't Terence but, at the same time, there was something familiar about it ...

'Look,' Beau said, 'I don't want to go back and tell Juanita she can't wear any of her new finery tonight. You come back with me and explain to her.'

Why not? I realized that I would be happier out of the flat for a while, even though the telephone was disconnected. As we walked past the television monitor for the front entrance, I glanced up at it uneasily. It showed only the immediate area around the door, though. Anybody could be lurking around the corner or across the street.

I was getting that beleaguered feeling again.

* * *

We got to the Happy Larry in time to have a leisurely drink before the show. What I was beginning to recognize as the usual crowd was already there. We caused a mild stir of excitement as we entered, largely, I suspected, because Beau and Juanita were with us.

Glasses were raised in salute and it took the merest nod of acknowledgement before they were clustering around us.

'I thought you boys just went to Closing Nights,' I said. That was where we had met them before.

'Oh, no,' Vic said. 'We're the Open and Shut Club. We come to Opening Nights and go to the Closings. That's one of the things we bet on: how long a show will last.'

'*One* of the things.' The voice was heavy with meaning and barely audible. It might have come from Mark.

'And whether it will transfer to the West End and how long it will last there.' It seemed to take very little to make Vic go a deep red.

'I'm Adam.' With a charming smile, he moved forward to cover Vic's confusion, and introduce the others. Mark, Greg and Paul shook hands like little gentlemen and made flattering remarks, especially to Juanita.

Only Ledbetter held back; shyly, I thought at first, then noticed that he was watching Beau and Juanita with a curious, almost appraising expression. Perhaps he didn't recognize Juanita, either.

A sudden gust of cloying scent engulfed us all. Heliotrope. My throat closed up and I noticed that I was not the only one to begin choking.

Evangeline muttered something under her breath that I hoped nobody else had heard.

Ledbetter and the others snapped to attention like a line of chorus boys when the star enters and the orchestra bursts into the hit song of the show. They hadn't done that with Evangeline and me, I noted bitterly; but perhaps we had lost our novelty value by being too easily available. We were just a couple of the boys now.

'Why, Beau, honey,' the saccharine voice trilled behind us. 'Beauregard Sylvester! I do declare!' The honeyed accents of the Old South began to make themselves apparent. 'Ah thought you were still on board the *Constellation!* When did you hit town?'

'You two starred together, didn't you?' Terence picked up his cue eagerly. 'In *The Heart-Throb of the Confederacy.*'

Better known to Hollywood insiders as *The Coronary of the Confederacy.* I thought Beau was going to have one on the spot.

'I thought you were going back to the States,' he growled.

'Oh, but you made London sound like such fun! And it is! It's so wonderful to see my dear old friends again.'

Evangeline growled. 'Sweetums looked us up. She said you gave her our address.'

'I thought she wanted to send a postcard.' Beau knew he was in trouble. His eyes rolled wildly. 'Juanita, you tell them.'

'Oh, is *this* Juanita?' Sweetums looked at her with frank disbelief. 'The *same* Juanita I saw two months ago? My dear, what have you been doing?'

'The cruise was very refreshing,' Juanita said. 'I had a good rest.'

'Really? You must give me his name.'

The warning bell sounded, making me, at any rate, jump. It sounded like the bell in a prize fight signalling the contenders to come out of their corners fighting.

'We'd better go upstairs,' I said. 'They're ready to start.'

'Plenty of time, plenty of time.' Barry Lane,

126

the landlord, materialized beside us, ice bucket and champagne in his hands.

'Oh, what a lovely surprise!' Sweetums simpered.

'The least I can do when such luminaries honour my establishment.' I was thankful he didn't say 'humble establishment,' that would have been carrying it too far. The look he shot the young men from under his lowered eyebrows made it clear that they were not included in the offer of free champagne.

'We ought to be getting upstairs.' Vic took the hint and started for the stairs with his friends. As they passed the entrance, I spotted a familiar head raised above the parapet of frosted glass to peer through the clear glass panel at the top of the door. It turned cautiously from side to side; its gaze rested for a moment on our group and then the head swerved and disappeared in the opposite direction.

The off-duty Superintendent Heyhoe was either going to use the public bar or patronize another pub altogether. We were more than he wanted to contend with tonight—even on a social level. Perhaps, especially on a social level.

'Why, Terence,' Sweetums giggled. I turned to see him refilling her glass. 'If I were ten years younger, I'd think you were trying to get me drunk.'

'Not even thirty years younger!' Evangeline muttered.

127

'I would if I could,' Terence replied gallantly, and more truthfully than he knew. It was rumoured that Sweetums had once drunk W. C. Fields under the table.

'Let's go see the show we're paying for.' Beau hauled Juanita roughly to her feet. I expected her to protest, but she seemed hardly to notice. From beneath her lowered lids, she looked at Beau, then at Sweetums, and then back to Beau again, as though trying to decide—not for the first time—just what, if anything, they had once been to each other.

Actually, she had no reason to worry. Beau had always had too good a sense of self-preservation to get too close to anyone as poisonous as Sweetums. However, it would do his morale a world of good if Juanita decided to throw a jealous fit over him.

The second bell rang with a peculiar intensity, suggesting that someone had seen Barry breaking out the champagne again and wanted to ensure that we remember we were there for the show.

'Take your glasses up with you,' Barry urged with the nervous air of a man who had been spoken to severely in the recent past. 'There'll be a fresh bottle of champagne waiting for you at the interval.'

I was behind the others as we started up the stairs. Just before the curve of the stairs took me out of the line of vision for the saloon bar below, I looked back.

At the far side of the room, the door into the public bar swung open and Heyhoe advanced cautiously into the saloon bar. An air of relief was apparent as he crossed over to Barry and began speaking. He had the field clear to himself until the interval when, presumably, he would retreat to the public bar again until all of us undesirables went upstairs for the second act.

The final bell sounded as we took our seats and settled down to watch the performance.

*   *   *

Gather Ye Rosebuds proved to be what once would have been called a revue, escaping that fate by a thin storyline linking the sketches and songs. The writers had obviously been traumatized by too many viewings of *Citizen Kane* and the end of every sketch was signalled by a sled with the name 'Rosebud' painted on it being drawn across the stage behind the actors. There were frequent sly—and sometimes lewd—references to W. R. and Marion and the real origin of the name.

However, it was bright and cheerful and a lot better than most of the shows we had seen lately. Sweetums was laughing it up far more than the rather feeble jokes called for, playing to the crowd, who laughed at her laugh, and paying no attention to the murderous looks

129

from the actors she was upstaging. Ah, well, if looks could kill, we'd have been free of Sweetums these many decades. She probably would never have made it past the first grade.

On the surface, there wasn't much in the show for us, but a couple of the songs were promising, one or two jokes were genuinely funny and it might be worth investigating just what the writers might have lying around in their desk drawers.

Rosebud tilted over on one side, revealing that it was outlined in little white lights and signalling the close of Act One. There was the usual rush for the exit, Beau and Juanita well to the front. Sweetums hung back, surrounded by the Open and Shut Club and relishing every moment of their attention.

'Hang on a minute,' I said to Evangeline. 'I just want to check something.' I squinted at the blurred and badly printed page of credits that passed for a programme.

Evangeline sank back in her seat with an impatient sigh. It was all right for her, she now had *Hamlet Swoons* to fall back on, stepping over Sweetums's dead body, if necessary. But if I wasn't going to get stuck playing a French maid, I still had to find something for myself, preferably a musical.

'Is everything all right?' an anxious voice asked.

'Just fine.' I looked up to see the rather charming face of one of the singers. Were they making the poor girl double as an usher? 'Thank you'—I squinted at the programme again—'Cara?'

'Cara Knowlton,' she affirmed. 'I'm so glad to have this chance to speak to you. I won't embarrass you, I'll just say I admire you both so much. Now, can I get you a drink or anything?'

'A little information, please.' I tilted the programme sideways, trying to decipher one of the names. 'That song—"Roses All Around Us"—was the same person responsible for both music and lyrics?'

'Oh, yes.' There was a betraying note of pride in her voice. 'Ewen Elliott. We think he's really talented.'

'So do I.' I could feel myself being carried along by her enthusiasm.

'Oh! Would you like to meet him? It would mean so much to him if you told him that yourself. I'll go and get—'

The piercing scream stopped her in her tracks as she turned away. Evangeline and I froze, then leapt to our feet.

There were shouts outside and a loud sickening thud. Then silence.

We dashed to the exit, Cara only a short length ahead of us, and crowded into the little hallway at the top of the stairs. Some of the audience were still on the stairs, but had pushed themselves back against the wall, staring down in horror.

131

'Sweetums—' Terence leaned over the banister, just two steps below us. 'Sweetums!' he cried brokenly.

But Sweetums was far more broken than he was. She lay motionless at the foot of the stairs, her head at an odd angle. She did not appear to be breathing.

Then, from somewhere in the distance beyond her, there was the distinct and unmistakable sound of a champagne cork popping.

* * *

Before we left the penthouse, Evangeline must have plugged in the telephone again. It was ringing when we opened the door. I closed the door and leaned against it, closing my eyes; I could not face one more thing tonight.

'I'll get it.' I heard Evangeline's footsteps cross the floor. 'Hello?'

There was a long silence. Eventually, I opened my eyes to see Evangeline replacing the receiver.

'Beau was right,' she said thoughtfully. 'We really must get this number changed.'

'Was it ... *him* again?'

'Probably. I certainly hope there aren't two of them around. He informed me that we had less than twenty-four hours. If we don't do the "decent thing" by midnight, he's coming after us.'

132

CHAPTER ELEVEN

'A sad loss...' Evangeline was paying tribute over the telephone when I entered the living room later, much later, that morning. 'Yes, I made one film with her. Practically everyone in the business worked with her ... once.'

I cleared my throat and rolled my eyes at her, reminding her that she was speaking to the media.

'It was a memorable experience.' Evangeline covered quickly, in the special voice she used for interviews—which had given me my clue. 'She was so vital, so spontaneous, so—' She allowed her voice to break huskily. 'So alive. Thank heavens she left so many brilliant films behind her. It's hard to believe we'll never see her again.'

I applauded silently as she replaced the phone.

'And they'd better hammer a stake through her heart to make sure of that,' Evangeline said, heading for the kitchen.

'Do you think we ought to leave the telephone plugged in?' I trailed after her, feeling somewhat jittery.

'Why not? We've already had our ultimatum. We've got until midnight to do the decent thing.'

'Whatever that is.'

'Yes, that's the problem, isn't it? What do you suppose someone like that would consider "the decent thing"?'

'The mind boggles.' I popped bread in the toaster while Evangeline absently attended to the coffee machine. It was the only time in the day when she pulled her weight in the kitchen, probably because she was never quite awake enough to notice she was doing it.

The doorbell startled me as I was setting our places at the table. I froze, staring in the direction of the entrance hall as though a ghost were about to materialize there. 'It couldn't be—'

'Of course not,' Evangeline said crossly. 'We have until midnight. Besides, that's the inside bell. Someone already in the building is ringing it.'

She was right, it was an inside job. The hammering on the door began before I was halfway across the living room, reinforced by Beau's hearty baritone.

'Evangeline! Trixie! You in there? You all right? Open the door!' There was a fresh burst of hammering.

'All right, all right, keep your shirt on. I'm coming!' I bellowed back at him. 'You needn't break the door down,' I said, opening it.

'I told you they were all right.' Juanita followed more placidly as Beau charged into the room. 'Why shouldn't they be?'

'I just wanted to make sure.' Beau was on the

134

defensive now. He looked at us half defiantly. 'Where the hell did you disappear to last night? I was going to wait for you after that policeman was finished with us, but he said you'd already left.'

'We had an alibi,' Evangeline said smugly. 'We were talking to one of the singers. We never went near the stairs at all.'

'Alibi?' Juanita lost her placidity. 'I do not like that word! Surely, what happened was an accident. Those stairs were dangerous.'

'Not as bad as some I've seen,' I said cheerfully.

'Yeah?' Beau glared at us. 'Well, this is the last time we go to a theatre with you two.'

I could live with that and so could Evangeline. She turned on her heel and started back to the kitchen.

'Come and have some coffee,' she called over her shoulder. 'You'll feel better.'

'Nothing will make me feel better.' He slumped down at the kitchen table and began gnawing at the piece of toast I'd just buttered for myself. 'You didn't see Sweetums the way I did. She landed practically at my feet. If I'd taken one more step down, I'd have stepped on her. And the noise she made—' he dropped the toast; suddenly it held no attraction for him.

'Just coffee, thank you.' If Juanita was troubled by intimations of mortality, she gave no sign of it.

Evangeline slammed the cup down in front

135

of her with, perhaps, more force than was necessary. Some of the liquid splashed over the side of the cup, flooding the saucer.

'And a fresh saucer,' Juanita murmured serenely.

'I think I could use some more toast.' Beau was recovering.

'Yes, madam. Yes, sir. Will that be all? We short-order cooks just live to serve!'

'I'll do the toast.' I rushed to the toaster, snapping at Evangeline out of the corner of my mouth, 'You *did* invite them, you know!'

'What the hell's the matter with you?' Beau stared at her in amazement.

'I am sorry.' Juanita was quicker on the uptake. 'We have been too long on board ship. It will take some time to readjust to a world in which everyone does not exist to do our bidding.'

Evangeline snorted and turned away.

'This is one helluva homecoming,' Beau brooded. 'First, no home to come back to, then Sweetums dying right at our feet like that. We shoulda stayed on the ship, or in Paris, even.'

'Incredible!' Evangeline said.

'You can say that again.' Beau grabbed eagerly for the fresh toast I brought over. 'I just can't believe that boy could get himself into such a financial fix.'

'Not Jasper,' Evangeline said. 'Sweetums.'

'Yes.' I knew what she meant. 'It is incredible to think of Sweetums Carew ending

136

up dying a natural death—when she's been asking for murder all her life.'

'Exactly!' Evangeline said.

'Now wait a minute,' Beau said nervously. 'I don't like that look in your eye. An accident counts as a natural death. At least, at Sweetums's age and loaded with champagne and fooling around at the top of a flight of stairs, it does.'

'Sweetums Carew was in the same age range as we are,' Juanita said. 'Whether she admitted it or not.' She did a little brooding herself.

'Yeah, but we stayed sober,' Beau said.

'I'm not sure that had anything to do with it.' Evangeline looked into the distance thoughtfully. 'Except that it made her an easier target for ... someone.'

'Evangeline!' I knew that look. It was the one she wore in *The Happy Couple* series just before she outwitted the stupid policeman in charge of the case yet again. 'Don't you dare even *think* such a thing!'

'I'm not the only one to suspect foul play. Why do you imagine Hoo-Ha kept asking everyone all those questions? And wasn't he disappointed'—Evangeline grinned—'when he discovered we had an iron-clad alibi?'

'I thought he was never going to let *us* go,' Beau said. 'He sure was anxious to pin something on somebody.'

'Did she fall or was she pushed?' Juanita was getting that faraway look, too. 'Was there not a

137

film of that title? Or was that the advertising line for it?'

'No!' I was surrounded by them. I started for the living room just as the doorbell rang.

'Now that *is* the outside bell,' Evangeline called after me. 'Be careful.'

'Why? What's the matter now?' Beau asked.

I checked the TV monitor, recognized the face staring up at the camera above the front door, and automatically pressed the lock-release button before I realized who it was.

'Oh, noooo!' I wailed. The situation had lacked only this.

'What is it?' Evangeline dashed into the room. 'Who is it?'

'Don't look now—' in fact, she couldn't, the face had disappeared from the tiny screen. He was already inside the building. I didn't want to tell her, but he was going to be at the door in another minute.

'Don't look now,' I repeated feebly. 'But we've just inherited Terence!'

At least, that got rid of Beau and Juanita. One look at Terence's woebegone face and they instantly remembered something terribly urgent they had to attend to back in Jasper's flat.

'I hope you don't mind my coming here like this,' Terence said, 'but I had to see you. Talk to you. You were her friends—' He broke off, struggling for control.

Evangeline and I carefully refrained from

138

looking at each other.

'Come and sit down and have a cup of coffee,' I said. Thank heaven we'd got all those new cups and saucers.

'Thank you.' He took several deep breaths as he followed us into the kitchen, making it sound as though we had a heavy breather right behind us. I tried not to worry about his sanity. Anyone who could be a fan of Sweetums...

'I'm sorry the others left,' he said. 'I'll want to talk to them, too.'

'I don't think they can tell you very much about Sweetums.' I was treading carefully in the face of his obvious grief. 'Neither can we. None of us have seen her for decades.'

'Oh, I don't need to hear anything like that,' he said. 'I know all about Sweetums Carew.'

I doubted that, but wasn't going to be the one to enlighten him further.

'No.' He accepted his coffee and sipped at it absently. 'No, I want to enlist your aid in planning her memorial service.'

'Memorial service?' Evangeline echoed faintly, sinking into a chair.

'Yes. A Tribute. A Celebration of her Life. I thought I'd—' He broke off, looking at us anxiously. 'Unless you'd like to organize it yourselves?'

Evangeline opened her mouth but, for once, nothing came out. She was struck speechless at the thought of organizing a celebration for the life of Sweetums Carew.

139

'Oh, we'd much rather leave that to you,' I said quickly, before she could get her breath back. 'We wouldn't know where to start.'

'With the church.' He relaxed. 'We—the Magnificent Stars of Yesteryear Fan Club— would book the church. Usually, it's St Paul's, Covent Garden—that's traditionally the actors' church. Or else St Martin-in-the-Fields, Trafalgar Square—they do a lot of memorial services too. Do you know if Sweetums would have had a preference?'

'Preference?' The mind boggled. I wasn't sure Sweetums would have recognized a church if she had fallen into one. 'No, I don't think so. I'm sure whichever you choose would have been all right with Sweetums.'

Evangeline began emitting little strangled whoops. Fortunately, Terence took them for signs of distress.

'Oh, I'm sorry,' he apologized. 'I didn't mean to upset you. It's probably much too soon to raise the subject, but one has to book the church so far in advance. I'm sorry, I didn't think. You knew her so well, even if it was such a long time ago. You were her friends. You must be absolutely devastated.'

Evangeline had regained control of her vocal cords, but her shoulders were still shaking, so was her entire body. She covered her face with her hands just in time.

'Perhaps we should talk about this later.' I stood up firmly. Hoping Terence would take his cue. 'I believe we *are* rather too upset to have a conversation about it right now.'

'Yes ... yes, of course.' He stumbled to his feet. 'I'm so sorry. I wasn't thinking...'

He was still apologizing as I closed the door behind him and went back to Evangeline, who was rolling about helplessly, tears streaming from her eyes.

'You. Are. Disgraceful!' Involuntarily, a giggle escaped me. Then another. In a moment, we were both whooping. I had got rid of Terence just in time.

'Devastated!' Evangeline dabbed at her eyes. 'Grief-stricken! Over Sweetums!'

'We'd better get it all out of our systems now.' I began to recover. 'We daren't twitch a muscle at the service. All those people from the fan club will be watching us.'

Suddenly, it wasn't funny at all any more.

'Yes.' Evangeline dried her eyes, completely serious now. Perhaps it had been a touch of hysteria that needed release. Actually being present at the sudden death of one of our colleagues, however much we disliked her, was unsettling to say the least.

'Oh, well.' Evangeline stood and began clearing the table. 'The show must go on.'

I was glad she didn't add, *Sweetums would have wanted it that way.*

*   *   *

141

Cold Dark Hearts at the Drawbridge wasn't bad. Unfortunately, it wasn't good, either. A long time ago, it would have had a modest run in a small Broadway theatre, earning back its operating nut and possibly making a small profit before going on the Straw Hat circuit and being released to amateur companies. But television had come along and scooped up all those sort of plays for fodder. It was kind of restful to see one again.

'They're talking about a West End transfer for this,' Ledbetter said. 'If they put it into one of the small intimate theatres, it might do well.'

The gang was all here. The minute we walked into the saloon bar downstairs, we had been hailed as old friends and buddies. Vic and Adam had come forward to greet us and invite us to join their party. Ledbetter looked up from his place in the corner with a beaming smile, which may have been for us or may have been because the others seemed to be showering him with money. He stuffed a large wad of bills into his pocket as he rose to greet us. Mark and Paul rushed to get chairs for us.

'The Sylvesters aren't coming tonight?' Greg looked around. 'They're all right, I hope.'

'They're fine,' I said. 'They just aren't as committed to the theatre as we are.'

'Oh, good.' He did not sound especially happy about it.

'Beau and Juanita are film stars first and last.' I tried to soften what appeared to be a

142

blow to him. 'Evangeline and I started out in the legitimate theatre. Despite all our films, it will always be our first love.'

Evangeline's snort made me aware that I was talking as though giving an interview—and also that 'legitimate' was hardly the word for the sort of performances we had been witnessing of late.

Champagne was offered, but we declined. Somehow, Sweetums's highpitched giggle was too associated with that drink.

'Brandy,' Evangeline said firmly. I agreed. Adam rushed off to get it.

The Drawbridge didn't have a bell, it had a buzzer. It was still annoying. I was beginning to long for a quiet evening undominated by bells, buzzers and the need to climb narrow rickety stairs to hard uncomfortable seats.

It was not until the momentary silence between the lights going down and the curtain rising that it occurred to me that no one had even mentioned Sweetums or referred to the night before. I didn't know whether to admire their tact or wonder if the whole episode had meant so little to their young lives that they had dismissed it already.

For once, the show wasn't all that bad. Perhaps being surrounded by personable young men added to our enjoyment. It was very pleasant to remain in our seats at the interval while willing minions dashed downstairs to get us fresh drinks.

143

Cold Dark Hearts even ended on an upbeat note, sending the audience out in a good mood. Perhaps it would do well in the West End. It was worth a try. However—an exchange of glances with Evangeline confirmed this—it had nothing to offer us. The playwright was not quite on our wavelength and unlikely to be in the foreseeable future.

Our clique escorted us downstairs in style. Vic and Adam went ahead of us, Mark and Paul followed behind, while Ledbetter and Greg acted as outriders on the side unprotected by the banister. It might have been flattering had I not suspected that the thought of Sweetums and her fate was not so far from their minds, after all.

'One for the road,' Vic suggested, a note of relief in his voice as we cleared the last step safely.

'Perhaps one,' Evangeline agreed. We allowed them to lead us back to the table in the corner. Vic and Adam went off to buy the drinks, returning in record time.

As everyone settled down around us with their drinks, I noticed Greg slipping a ten-pound note to Ledbetter.

'Stake-holding again?' Evangeline hadn't missed it, either. 'Can anyone join your game? I wouldn't mind a little flutter myself.'

'Oh, no!' Ledbetter started convulsively, shocked horror on his face. 'No, you don't want to join in this sweepstake. You wouldn't

144

like it at all.'

'No, you mustn't,' Vic agreed uncomfortably. 'It isn't in very good taste.' Suddenly embarrassment was palpable in the air.

Evangeline quirked an eyebrow at me and I quirked one back at her. What could they be betting on? And how sweet of the dear boys to want to protect our innocence. Obviously they had never heard the stories of some of the wilder Hollywood parties where drunken moguls won bets by having dim-witted starlets measure out their manhood by balancing quarters along the length of their—

'There they are!' The door burst open and a raving maniac erupted into the room, all but foaming at the mouth.

'There they are, the dirty bitches!' He charged straight at us, heedless of the placating figure making soothing noises just behind him.

Vic and Adam pushed back their chairs in alarm and stood ready to defend us. It was as well we had the table between us and the wild-eyed maniac.

'They used to hang people like you where you came from!' he howled. 'They hung horse thieves!'

'Dorsal! Dorsal! Take it easy!' Brendan plucked at his friend's elbow unheeded.

'They knew how to treat horse thieves!' he thundered. 'Hang them! Hang them!'

I wasn't sure how horses got into this, but I

145

recognized the enthusiasm for hanging. 'You're the one who's been telephoning us.'

'You're early.' Evangeline glanced at her watch. 'It isn't midnight yet.'

'I'll teach you to laugh, you filthy—' He lunged across the table, but Vic and Adam caught him and pulled him back.

'Steal a man's best friend and laugh in his face,' he ranted. 'Hanging's too good for you. Give me back The Semtex!'

CHAPTER TWELVE

'Semtex!!!'

Shock loosened the grip our would-be protectors had on Dorsal Finn and he shook them off, leaning forward menacingly.

'Give him back! You've no right to him! I want him now or I want your blood! I want The Semtex!'

'Nova!' I said.

'Lucy!' Evangeline exclaimed.

Talk about wild surmise. We looked at each other, then looked at the outraged face glowering at us.

'The Curse of Finn be on ye for your treacherous deed,' he intoned. 'Ye'll have no peace. I'll haunt you night and day. I'll set a blood-curse on you down to generations yet unborn—'

146

'Oh, shut up!' Evangeline said. 'We haven't got your damned dog!'

'Dog?' Vic looked relieved but puzzled. 'Is that what this is all about? What about the Semtex?'

'That's what they were fool enough to name the hound.' Evangeline looked Dorsal Finn straight in his blazing eyes. 'His name is Tex now—and he's a lot happier with it.'

'There! You admit it! You've got him! And you've even changed his name! You're keeping him prisoner from me! You—'

'Dorsal, Dorsal.' Brendan caught him by the shoulders and eased him into the chair Adam had vacated. 'Give them a minute to gather themselves together. You've burst in on them out of the blue. Give them a chance to explain themselves. They've already said they haven't got The Semtex.'

'Where is he then?' Even sitting, Dorsal was like a coiled spring. 'The last we saw, you'd bundled him into a taxi and were making off with him like thieves in the night. We ran after you, but we couldn't stop you. You—'

'Your dog followed us,' I corrected coldly. 'He shoved his way into the taxi with us and wouldn't get out.'

'So you took him!' Dorsal was unrelenting. 'And you've kept him. He's a valuable animal, you know. Worth who knows how many thousands. He's in direct descent from the wolfhounds who ran with the early Celtic

147

Kings of Ireland.'

'I'd like to read that on his Kennel Club papers before I believe it,' Evangeline muttered. I kicked her ankle under the table; Dorsal was calming down a bit and we didn't want to start him off again. For one thing, I didn't think Ledbetter's nerves could take it; he was quite pale and had developed a distressing twitch.

The bartender had been keeping a vigilant eye on our corner, now I saw him reach overhead and do something with one hand. The lights flickered suggestively. 'Last orders, please!' he called.

'They're closing.' The thrill of hope faded almost immediately as I recognized the snag in that.

'I want The Semtex—and I want him now!' Dorsal Finn crashed his fist down on the tabletop.

'I told you, we don't have him,' Evangeline said crossly. 'But'—she hesitated—'I think we know where he is.'

'Think! You mean you don't know? You've stolen my dog and lost him!'

'He's not lost.'

'Where is he, then?'

'That is,' Evangeline amended carefully. 'We know who has him.'

'So, who has him? And where are they?'

That was the snag. They knew where we lived, but we didn't know where Nova and

148

Lucy lived. The only way we could reach them was at the pub where Lucy worked. And it was closing time for pubs. The place would be dark and deserted by the time we could get there.

'I believe you'll find him at the Emperor Uncloth'd tomorrow night.'

'And where is that when it's at home?'

'Oh, you must know—' Evangeline waved a hand vaguely and I realized that she didn't know. Neither did I. Nova had driven us a long winding way; we had no idea of the address. We had only one clue: 'By the canal.'

'There now, Dorsal,' Brendan said quickly. 'That's fine, isn't it? We'll go there tomorrow as soon as they open and collect The Semtex. Sure, he'll be glad to see you again after all his adventures. We'll have the grand reunion and it will all be fine.'

'It better be.' Dorsal still regarded Evangeline suspiciously. 'I'm warning you. I'll have me dog—or I'll have your lives!'

'That's enough of that!' The bartender had come up behind him quietly. 'We don't want you and your threats around here.'

'It wasn't a threat,' Brendan defended quickly. 'More just a warning, like.'

'In front of witnesses,' Evangeline pointed out.

'Your taxi has arrived, ladies,' the bartender said. 'It's waiting outside. I'll just make sure these boyos stay here until you're well clear.'

'What a good idea.' Evangeline and I moved

quickly. Vic and Adam escorted us to Eddie's waiting taxi while Mark, Greg, Paul and Ledbetter stayed in place to reinforce the bartender in case of trouble.

I wasn't sure how much help Ledbetter would be. Looking back, I saw him slump in his chair and mop at his brow with a handkerchief nearly as white as his forehead.

*   *   *

We slept late the next morning; we deserved it. For once, I was the first one up and able to enjoy the quiet luxury of having breakfast alone with the morning newspaper. The world seemed pretty much in its usual state, with incomprehensible wars being fought in places I couldn't even pronounce ... politicians wrangling over obscure grievances disguised as points of law ... libellous interpretations of American foreign policy decisions ...

In the bottom right-hand corner of the front page, I saw the picture. It was a publicity shot I had seen many times across the years with only the caption varying. This time it was the final caption: 'Sir Gervaise Cordwainer Dies.' I skimmed the short paragraphs: 'Peacefully in his sleep ... at his manor house in Sussex ... aged 96 ... long illustrious career ... see Obituaries, page 14.'

I felt the pang you get when the living legends slip away. What made it worse was that

I hadn't realized he was still alive. I'd worked with him once during the few years he spent in Hollywood, accepting every part that was offered as he struggled to rack up some capital for his declining years. He had played my grandfather, a titled snob horrified because his granddaughter insisted on going on the stage. In the end, of course, he had been won round and even wound up doing a soft-shoe finale with me to close the film.

I heard a sigh and knew that it was mine. A piece of my own history had just slipped away, too.

'What's the matter?' Evangeline had appeared silently in the doorway. 'Why all the sighing?'

Wordlessly, I handed her the page.

'Oh.' She sank down into the chair opposite me, 'He was in two plays with me in the West End. He played my father in *Briefer Candles* and my much-older diplomat husband in *Diplomatic Immunity*.' She gave a sigh of her own. 'We had a lot of laughs together. I hadn't realized the old boy was still alive.'

'He isn't ... now.' We both sighed. *Never send to know for whom the bell tolls* ...

'Oh, no!' Evangeline had been turning the page swiftly, now she paused. 'It's one of the new-type obituaries. More warts than all. How disgraceful!' But I noticed she was reading avidly.

'Hah!' she said, coming to the end of the

151

obit. 'There were at least three more mistresses they've missed.' She sounded much too happy about it; I wondered if she had been one of them. It was not really a question I could ask her; if I did, she'd only lie.

The telephone rang and Evangeline got up to answer, arranging her face into a suitable expression of restrained sorrow.

'I suppose that's Rent-a-Quote,' she said. She marched into the living room and I heard her voice change from a rather funereal tone to a pleased coo.

'Why, Victor, dear, how sweet of you. We'd be delighted ... Oh ...' Her voice changed, she was not quite so delighted now. 'Well, I don't know. I can't speak for Beau and Juanita, of course. You'll have to ask them yourself.'

I picked up my cup and saucer and wandered into the living room. Evangeline made a face at me.

'Oh, all right,' she said. 'I'll try to persuade them. Perhaps I can bring them round.' She rolled her eyes heavenwards. 'Yes, yes, I'll do my very best. All right ... goodbye.' She slammed the phone down violently.

'Persuade them!' she said. 'As soon as Beau hears it's a free meal, there'll be no holding him back!'

'You didn't seem exactly shy about it yourself. Mind telling me what's going on?'

'We're dining with Vic and the Open and Shut Club at the Queen and Country
152

tomorrow night. They want Beau and Juanita to come along, too.'

'The Queen and Country? Isn't that where we saw that awful thing where they kept killing everybody in sight? Umm...' Then I had it. '*Farewell, Everyone?*'

'Vic says that's finished now. The new show starts tomorrow night and is included in our evening out with them: *The Mist in the Meadow*. That sounds a lot better. Gentler... dreamy...'

'Uh-huh.' I was not persuaded. Any pub that could put on *Farewell, Everyone* was not to be trusted in its choice of future productions. The title might sound innocuous but...

'Let's see what Beau and Juanita say.' I was going to place my trust in Beau's wariness. Hadn't he just recently told us he'd never go to another pub performance with us again?

* * *

So much for my faith in any statement of Beau's. His parsimony won, as Evangeline had known it would. The prospect of a free meal and show braced him against any prospect of a nightmare performance. After the amount of food and drink he took on board, he could easily sleep through it.

I didn't consider the food to be all that good, but I've had worse, I think. This pub, like all

153

the others, specialized in what was now traditional English Fayre, which translated into lasagne, moussaka and steak-and-kidney pie—with plenty of chips with everything.

Everybody else seemed to be having such a good time that I hated to spoil the fun by seeming to suggest that my steak-and-kidney pie tasted even worse than usual—I never did like kidney. I pushed the offending bits to one side and soldiered on. Once in a while, I glanced at Juanita's plate and noticed that unidentifiable objects were being ostracized from the rest of her moussaka and piled in a grisly heap at the side of her plate.

Evangeline and Beau ate everything. They would. It was free. Evangeline had some nerve to talk about Beau being cheap.

'Something wrong?' Ledbetter had noticed that I was picking at my food. 'If you don't like it, leave it. We'll get you something else.'

'That's right.' Greg half rose, reaching for my plate. 'How about the lasagne?' They looked at me nervously; this was their treat and I was in danger of spoiling the party.

'Oh, no. No, it's all right.' I made a special effort and speared a small piece of beef and a large chunk of crust dripping with gravy. 'It's just fine, honestly. I'm not very hungry, that's all.'

Actually, I'd lost my appetite a couple of hours ago, when the telephone calls started again. It was all right for Evangeline, she

154

hadn't answered the phone.

I'd done so without thinking. The long silence at the other end of the line gradually told me what a mistake I'd made. Just as I was about to hang up, he'd spoken: 'You rotten bitches! I'm coming for you!' Then he'd slammed the phone down at his end.

'What's the matter?' Evangeline had looked up as I caught my breath and felt myself swaying. The hatred and menace in his voice had caught me by surprise.

'It's that Irishman again.' I had replaced the phone and sunk into the nearest chair. 'He says he's coming for us. He ... he sounds like he means it.'

'What's the matter with that fool now?' It was too bad Evangeline hadn't answered the phone, her irritation would have been enough to discourage any madman. 'He's got his rotten dog back.' A second thought occurred to her. 'Hasn't he?'

'How do I know? But it might be worth finding out.' I looked around for the telephone directory. 'Maybe we ought to call that pub and talk to Lucy.'

'Lucy...' Evangeline's eyes narrowed. 'I thought she was making too much of a fuss over the great beast. You don't suppose...?'

The landlord at the Emperor Uncloth'd confirmed that *The Crumbl'd Wall* had closed on Saturday night. Lucy had been employed by the theatre company and not the pub, he had

155

no idea where she might be now. And no, he didn't know where *The Crumbl'd Wall* was going to be showing next.

'That's it!' I replaced the phone. 'Dorsal went over there to get his dog back, found everybody had disappeared without trace—and he blames us. He said...' My voice quavered. 'He said ... he's coming for us.'

'Bluster and bravado!' Evangeline dismissed Dorsal's threats. 'Nothing but noise and—'

'He's awfully mad.' She hadn't heard the depths of violence in his voice. 'He said,' I repeated, just in case she hadn't taken it in the first time, 'he was coming for us. And he meant it.'

'Then isn't it fortunate that we have an engagement elsewhere this evening?' ...

And now she sat there, without a care in the world, shovelling down a mess indigestible enough to make a camel collapse.

The first bell sounded and Juanita leaped to her feet, pushing aside her plate.

'I wish to choose my seat,' she declared. 'I do not like always arriving at the last minute and taking what is left over.'

'Speaking of leftovers—' Beau was already reaching for her plate. 'If you're not going to finish this, I will.'

Juanita closed her eyes and shuddered. 'He will pay for this tonight,' she murmured. I didn't know whether she meant in indigestion or in being nagged, but that was Beau's little

156

problem. Juanita had already solved mine.

'Yes, I hate that last-minute rush myself.' I, too, rose and pushed aside my plate. I was relieved that Evangeline did not offer to finish it. 'Let's get upstairs and get good seats.'

I didn't really feel it was necessary for Adam and Vic to escort us but, apparently, they did. It put a stop to any complaints Juanita and I might have exchanged.

The room seemed larger than before, but that might have been an optical illusion due to the fact that none of the seating was stationary. Rows of fold-up chairs fanned out across the room, not always in orderly lines.

A large black curtain had been dragged across the slightly raised stage, but one could see behind it at the side. I noted an ominous-looking black contraption and my heart sank. There was obviously going to be a mist in *The Mist in the Meadow*. I wondered how experienced the stagehands were at handling a smoke machine, especially one that looked as outdated and second-, third-, or even fourth-hand as that one.

'I think I'll sit here.' I chose a chair at the end of the third row; a few steps would carry me to the exit.

'But you won't be able to see so well there,' Vic objected. 'Why not come back to the middle of one of the centre rows?'

'This is fine.' I knew what I was doing, but wasn't tactless enough to explain my real reasons. 'Actually, I'm not feeling too well. If I have to slip out during the performance, I don't want to be climbing over people and disturbing everyone.'

'I will remain with my friend.' Juanita firmly plumped herself down next to me. 'If she is not feeling well, I will see to her.' She gave the boys one of her enchanting smiles, which was at full power again now that her face had been fixed.

'If you're sure...' Vic said doubtfully.

'You're very thoughtful.' Adam gazed at Juanita with something close to adoration.

Just then the others appeared in the doorway and moved towards us. Vic waved a hand, directing them towards what he considered to be the choice seats in the middle of the room. Beau hesitated as he passed us. He looked from Juanita to Adam and a deep frown wrinkled his forehead. He hadn't missed that look on Adam's face. He moved to go past us and take the seat beside Juanita, but Adam nipped in and got it first. Beau's frown deepened, he moved on, but not very far. He settled himself in the end seat just a couple of rows behind us—where he could keep an eye on his wife and her admirer.

Evangeline quite happily allowed herself to be led to a centre seat where she was surrounded by her own admiring coterie.

After a brief behind-scenes battle, the curtain was jerked aside and *The Mist in the Meadow* started—in more ways than one. It

158

was a ghost story, as I might have suspected. A table with a gas lamp on it, a shabby red Victorian sofa and a couple of chairs stood at the opposite side of the stage to me. A fragment of plasterboard, waist-high, indicated an outside wall separating the nineteenth-century parlour from the meadow outside.

A man and a woman walked into the parlour; the man settled himself in an armchair; the woman crossed to stand beside the gas lamp, looking beyond it, through what was obviously meant to be a window. There was something vaguely familiar about her.

'It's so dark out there,' she began. 'So cold ... and so lonely ... and the mist is rising. On a night like tonight, I cannot help remembering...'

'Don't!' The man surged to his feet and rushed to her, catching her arm and pulling her roughly away from the window. 'Don't talk like that! Don't brood! Don't ... remember!'

I turned and caught Evangeline sending me a triumphant look. She was very pleased with herself for getting closer to the onstage action. I leaned back and bided my time. We would see.

'You can't shut it out!' the woman cried, as the man mimed drawing the curtains. 'It's in here already. Inside of us!'

He had pulled her clear of the table and I studied her costume idly—until I got to her shoes. My eardrums gave an anguished throb.

159

I recognized her now. I hoped she wasn't going to do much screaming in this production.

'Treexie—' Beside me, Juanita sniffed sharply and leaned closer to whisper. 'Do you smell fire?'

'It's all right.' I gestured towards our corner of the stage where white clouds were beginning to billow out from the antiquated piece of machinery being worked by two blackclad figures in the wings. 'I think.'

'You theenk they know what they are doing?' In the stress of the moment, her accent thickened.

I wished she hadn't asked me that. Surely, the 'mist' was swooping across the stage much too quickly. And wasn't there a faintly desperate air about the black-clad duo working the machine? My stomach gave a nervous lurch.

'The mist is rising out in the meadow,' the woman said, on a rising note herself. 'It seems to be coming from...' She had wrenched the curtains open again. 'From the spot where ... where...'

'Don't!' The man's dialogue was a bit limited, so he was trying to make up for that by a lot of body language or, as we used to say, chewing the scenery. Not that there was much scenery to chew in this production. He grabbed her by the shoulders and forced her back towards the sofa. I wouldn't like to have her bruises in the morning.

160

The 'mist' was hot on his heels, rolling across the stage ankle-deep and rising, spreading out in all directions. In the front row, someone stifled a cough.

'It's waiting out there in the mist . . .' She was overoptimistic, if you ask me, considering that the mist was rapidly engulfing them where they stood.

'Imagination!' The man cast a worried look over his shoulder, obviously the script did not call for the mist to advance so rapidly.

I followed his gaze, to find the shadowy figures disappearing into the fog at their end. One of them appeared to be on his knees, wrestling with the orifice of the machine, trying to point it in another direction. The other figure was bent over it, hands clenched into fists and hammering silently at it. It continued to belch out smoke, fog and mist with even more enthusiasm than before.

The actors were hip-deep in the stuff now and fighting panic as they realized they might soon be invisible. Worse, the uncontrolled fog was eddying out into the auditorium, threatening the audience. There were more coughs, not so stifled this time, and the rustle of feet shifting uneasily.

'Don't thwart me, Ephraim!' The voice soared out, as though realizing that soon it might be the only beacon in the disappearing surroundings. The mist was waist-high now; it was a solid rolling bank of fog at our end of

161

the stage.

'You'll not open the door!' he shouted. 'You'll not let that mist into the house!'

That raised a few titters, since there was now not a corner to which the mist had not penetrated. I saw several inhalers being produced and wielded with varying degrees of surreptitiousness. Other people began dabbing at their suddenly teary eyes.

In the wings, it was all hands to the pump. Two more figures, not bothering with any attempt at camouflage, had joined the original two dark shadows. They all battled with the smoking contraption, but the only thing clear was that they were doomed to lose the battle.

'Air!' I gasped, beginning to choke as the mist enveloped us. 'I need air. I'm getting out of here!' I dashed for the exit sign, which was already blurred, losing all brightness and definition in the rising fog.

There were footsteps immediately behind me. Juanita, I presumed. She wasn't one to stay and suffer when there was a means of escape close by. I wondered if Evangeline was so pleased with her choice of seat now.

I plunged down the stairs and kept on going, across the saloon bar, which I could barely see through streaming eyes, out of the door leading to the street, and to the edge of the pavement before I stopped under the streetlamp, half sobbing and gasping in the clear fresh air.

'There you are!' a voice roared behind me. 'I've got you, you scheming bitch! Now you're for it!'

Long, thin, icy fingers closed around my neck and tightened like a coil of steel.

CHAPTER THIRTEEN

I raised my hands to claw feebly at the relentless hands tightening around my throat, cutting off my breath. Why had I trimmed my fingernails the other day? I was helpless. I felt consciousness begin to slip away from me.

I heard a shout from what seemed a long distance away and the sound of running feet. Then a babble of voices, but so far away ... so far away ...

'See here, what do you think you're doing?' It was Adam's voice, faint and lightweight, half afraid to offend anyone—even a killer. 'See here, old man, calm down and let's talk this over.'

'UNHAND THAT WOMAN!' The bellow of rage loosened the fingers that had been intent on strangling me.

Beau, I recognized thankfully. Dear old Beau, presented with a situation he had faced in myriad films, knew just what to do when he saw a frail blonde being menaced.

I felt the hands being wrenched away from

163

my neck. I opened my eyes in time to see Dorsal Finn being raised bodily off the ground and held aloft.

'Don't you—' For good measure, Beau began shaking him. 'Ever. Ever. Put your dirty hands on one of my friends again!'

He raised Dorsal still higher and hurled him across the road. There was a thud as Dorsal hit the ground and lay motionless.

'I say!' an awestruck voice whispered.

'They said he never used a double in his action shots.' Vic whistled softly. 'He didn't need to. He still doesn't.'

'Oh, Beau!' I fought for breath and gazed at him incredulously. 'You saved my life!' I hoped he didn't notice the unflattering amazement in my voice; I didn't mean it that way. I was just so astounded. And thankful.

'Aw, shucks!' Beau could do the rest of the dialogue for this scene in his sleep. 'It was nothin', ma'm. Trixie.'

'He can't be the age they give in the record books.' Ledbetter's emotions seemed thoroughly mixed, admiration and jealousy and an odd note of complaint. 'It must be true, what they say about theatre people: first they take years off to make themselves younger, then they add years on to get credit for being so spry when they're so old.' He seemed to be having a problem with the thought.

'It was wonderful, Beau.' I didn't grudge him his accolade. '*You* were wonderful! You're

164

a hero!'

'He is always a hero, my Beauregard,' Juanita purred, curling against him like a cat.

'Aw, shucks,' Beau said again. He kept his head lowered modestly, but I'll swear his chest expanded at least six inches. He put his arm around Juanita, losing track of which woman he had rescued.

Not that I wanted a romantic clinch with Beau. Across the street, I saw Dorsal roll over on to his stomach and begin to crawl away slowly. I kept my mouth shut. I didn't want another scene with him, either.

Behind us, coughing and spluttering, the rest of the audience was spewing out on to the pavement. It was too early for the interval; it looked like everybody else was abandoning ship, too.

'What's happened?' Evangeline reeled over to us, picking up on the atmosphere immediately. 'What have I missed?'

'Nothin', really.' Beau was still being modest.

'Beau has been wonderful.' I gave him his due.

'He has?' Evangeline regarded us sharply, then decided that Juanita was looking far too contented for her first interpretation of the dialogue to be correct. 'In what way?'

'I'll tell you later,' I said.

'Let's get outa here,' Beau said. 'I've had enough of tonight. I never shoulda let you talk

165

me into this. Although it was damn lucky for Trixie that I did.'

'You can say that again,' I agreed. I could have died while our English hosts were trying to use sweet reasonableness on Dorsal.

'Home,' Juanita throbbed, arching against Beau. 'Yes, I want to take my hero home ... and bathe his wounds ... and tell him how wonderful he is ... and sing him to sleep.'

Suddenly, I saw how she had stayed married to him all these years, despite her ruined face. When the lights are out ...

'TAXI!' Beau waved his arm at a taxi cruising down the street. 'Come on, all you girls—' He herded us into the taxi. 'Let's go home.'

*   *   *

'How are you feeling?' Evangeline asked when I appeared in the kitchen late the next morning.

'How do you expect?' I rubbed gingerly at my sore throat and slumped into a chair at the table.

'I made hot chocolate for you.' Evangeline filled a cup at the stove and brought the steaming fragrant brew over to me. 'Use lots of cream. It will be good for your throat.'

'We've got to get that damned dog back.' I had been giving the matter some thought in the wakeful moments between nightmares all night. 'Or that maniac will kill us both.'

'Never mind that.' Evangeline had her own

166

agenda. 'Lucy and Nova have walked off with *my* play.'

'The Irishman's dog and your play.' A gloomy foreboding swept over me. 'Your unfinished play. They'll be lying low now until Lucy finishes it.' By which time, they would probably hope that we would have forgotten all about the dog. 'We may never see them again.'

The thought should have cheered me, but it seemed as though nothing could do that this morning. I looked down at my cup of chocolate; it smelled delicious. I took a small sip; my throat said yes, my stomach said no. I put the cup down again.

'Would you like some toast?' Evangeline was watching me, a trace anxiously.

I shook my head. The thought of rough scratchy toast—I raised my hand to my throat.

'You could dunk it,' she suggested. 'That would soften it, so that you could manage it, all soft and squidgy—'

I pushed back my chair and dashed for the bathroom...

When I returned, Evangeline surveyed me critically. 'There are bruises on your throat.'

'I'm not surprised.' I perched on the end of my chair, not sure how long I was going to sit there. The smell of the chocolate wafted up to my nostrils and suddenly it didn't smell so good any more. I pushed at my cup. 'For heaven's sake, take this away!'

167

'Would you like anything else?' Evangeline whisked it out of sight. 'Tea? Coffee?'

I shuddered.

'Should I call the doctor?'

'We don't have a doctor.'

'I'll ring Jasper. He must know of one around here.' She started for the phone.

'Stop fussing and sit down!' I don't often snap and she almost fell into her chair with surprise. She looked at me closely.

'Everyone is entitled to an off day,' she said.

'Thanks!' Especially after they'd been throttled, not to mention all that smoke inhalation.

'Why don't you go back to bed?'

'I ... might ... just ... do that.' The idea held a lot of appeal. Suddenly, I wanted nothing more than to lie down and rest, even if I didn't sleep.

'And take a couple of aspirins. Soluble ones,' she added quickly as I raised a hand to protest. 'You can drink those down without any difficulty.'

'Soluble aspirin...' I tested the idea gingerly. There was no strong response one way or the other from my stomach. 'I suppose that can't do any harm.'

She mixed the aspirin and brought it to me. I was just raising the glass to my lips when the telephone rang, startling me so that I nearly dropped the glass.

'You plugged it in again!' I accused,

168

almost whimpering.

'I'll get it.' The grim set of Evangeline's mouth boded ill for any caller who was looking for a fight—or a dog.

'Oh, it's you.' I heard her voice relax, then change into a differently aggressive tone. 'I suppose you're not calling to tell us that Hugh has found a play for us? Or a theatre?'

'Martha!' I found new strength to bring me to my feet and carry me into the living room. 'All right, Evangeline, I'll take it.'

'No, I thought not.' She swerved, evading my outstretched hand.

'It's for me. Give it to me!' I lunged for the phone, but was brought up sharply by a stitch in my side.

'Evangeline—' I sank down on the sofa, clutching at my side. 'Give me the phone.'

'I don't know why your mother wants to speak to you,' Evangeline said coldly. 'No play. No theatre. You have nothing to say to us.'

I caught hold of the cord and yanked the receiver from her hand. 'Martha, darling, how are you?'

'Mother! I was afraid that wretched creature wasn't going to let me speak to you. I've been trying to reach you for days. Where have you been?'

'Oh ... in and out ... round and about,' I said vaguely. 'We're doing a lot of theatregoing these evenings.' It sounded better than

169

pub-crawling.

'That explains it. I've been ringing in the evenings; I'm so busy during the day, getting the children settled at school, redoing the house, meeting Hugh for lunch with his friends...' She sounded so happy.

'That's all right, dear. I know you're busy.' Evangeline was making faces again. I turned my back to her.

'Tell her not to bother wasting any of her valuable time on us—' Evangeline pitched her voice to carry. 'And that goes for her precious husband, too. We're finding our own show.'

'What was that?' Martha cried. 'What did she say? It was something nasty, wasn't it?'

'It usually is,' I sighed. 'Look, Evangeline—' I turned back to her. 'Why don't you—?'

'All right, all right. I'm just leaving.' Evangeline threw up her hands. 'I have better things to do than stand around listening to boring conversations. I'm going out.'

'Where?' I was instantly suspicious. 'No, no, not you, Martha. Just a minute, I'm saying something to Evangeline.'

'I hope it's goodbye!' Martha snapped.

'Out,' Evangeline said. 'Just ... out.' She gave me her most maddening smile.

'Evangeline! You're not to go anywhere near Kilburn! It isn't safe! Besides, Nova and Lucy don't live there—they're farther out. Nova said so—and she didn't specify in which direction.'

'Mother! What's going on? Are you all right?

170

What do you mean, not safe?'

'It's all right, Martha. Nothing's wrong.' I tried to soothe her and keep track of Evangeline at the same time.

Ignoring my protestations, Evangeline vanished into her bedroom and returned wearing her coat and drawing on her gloves. She made a beeline for the door.

'Wait a minute—' I called after her. 'Let me get dressed. I'm coming with you.'

'You're not well enough.' She paused at the door and looked back. 'Have a nice gossip with Martha and then go back to bed.'

'No, wait—' But the door closed behind her and she was gone. In the perverse way that such things happen, I immediately heard the clash of the lift doors and the whine of the motor. Today of all days, it had to be waiting at our floor to facilitate her escape.

'Mother, what is it?' Martha's anxious voice recalled me to the moment.

'Nothing, dear.' There was no point in worrying her; there was nothing she could do about it, either. 'Evangeline has just gone out … to do some errands.'

Abstractedly, I watched the front door TV monitor as Evangeline left the building, just as Nigel was about to enter. They stopped to talk and I saw Evangeline curl a predatory hand around his arm as she gazed into his eyes and spoke earnestly. He nodded his head with a slightly glazed look and together they walked

171

out of range of the monitor.

'Now, darling.' I turned back to Martha with a feeling of relief. Evangeline had found herself an escort for the afternoon. 'Tell me how the children are settling down in school...'

I felt a lot better by the time we finished our conversation, perhaps even well enough to have some tea and toast before retiring for a nap. My stomach stayed quite calm at this thought; it didn't lurch until the telephone rang again abruptly.

'Yes, dear?' I picked it up with a false sense of security, having instantly convinced myself that Martha must have remembered something else she wanted to tell me.

'Flee for yer lives, I'm warning yer! Himself is on the loose and out of control!'

'Brendan.' It could be no one else. 'Thank you for the warning, but you're a little late. I had a run-in with Dorsal Finn last night.'

'And you're alive to tell the tale?' he marvelled. 'Sure, you must have the luck of the Irish yourself. He was that furious, I was sure he'd kill.'

'He did his best.' I stroked my throat lightly. 'If he ever comes near me—or Evangeline—again, I'll see to it that he spends a very long time in jail.'

'Ah, now, you wouldn't do that? He's just high-spirited, is all. And don't forget, you started it. It was all your fault. You never

172

should have done it.'

'We did nothing!' Sheer irritation straightened my back and quickened my breathing. I realized I was beginning to feel a lot better. 'That man attacked me without cause or provocation!'

'"Cause", say you? "Provocation", say you? That depends on how you look at it. I'd say no one has the right to come between a man and his dog.'

'Come between? That dog made its own choice—and a damned sensible one, I'd say! We didn't ask it to follow us. We didn't give it any encouragement at all. We didn't even know it was there. When we discovered it, we tried to send it back. Nova and Lucy were supposed to deliver it back to him. Try finding them and you'll get Tex back.'

'Nova who? And Lucy who?'

He had me there. I realized that I couldn't remember their last names if, indeed, I had ever known them. Perhaps Evangeline knew, but she wasn't here now.

'*You* shouldn't have any trouble finding out who they are and where they live.' A counterattack is the best defence. 'You live here and you know more about the pub scene than we do.'

'And Tex, is it now?' A change of subject to deflect the attack isn't bad, either. 'If the poor miserable creature is nothing to you, since when have you taken it upon yourself to

173

change his name?'

'Since anyone could see "the poor miserable creature" cringe every time anyone called him "The Semtex". It was a damned stupid name for a dog—you ought to have been reported to the RSPCA!'

'Ah, now. Ah, now.' He recanted hastily. ''Twas Himself as named him. You've got to make allowances for the artistic temperament.'

'No, I haven't. Especially when there's no artistry in it.'

'You think not?' He didn't sound as though the thought came as a complete shock to him. 'You don't acknowledge Dorsal Finn as one of the great undiscovered geniuses of our time, then?'

I let the silence build while I mentally debated the choice between giving him the horse-laugh or just hanging up quietly.

'Are you still there?' he asked finally, an uncertain tremor in his voice.

'Not for much longer...'

'No, no! Don't ring off yet!' His voice rose in panic. 'We need to talk—'

'Maybe *you* need to talk, but I need to go and lie down. I'm recovering from a brutal physical attack last night.'

'Oh, God! Oh, God! I'll kill him when I find him again! Where did you say you saw him last?'

'I didn't say.' And I wasn't sure it would be safe to tell him. Despite the fervour in his voice,

174

he was exaggerating, of course. Or was he? To anyone in constant contact with Dorsal Finn, the thought of murdering him must present an ever-present temptation.

'But you're going to.' The voice took on a coaxing, wheedling note. ''Tis the last clue we have to his whereabouts. If I don't find him, he may have another go at you. You wouldn't want that.'

'No.' He was right; I wouldn't. 'The last I saw of Dorsal Finn, he was crawling on his hands and knees along the gutter across the street from the Queen and Country.'

'The gutter, you say? What was he doing there?'

'It was where he landed when Beauregard Sylvester prized his hands from around my throat and threw him across the street.'

'Threw him across the street?' There were several gasps and choking sounds. 'Into the gutter? That's an insult that can only be avenged in blood!'

'It will be *his* blood, if Beau ever gets his hands on him again. If he knows what's good for him, he'll keep away from us—all of us.'

'But where is he now?'

'I don't know and I don't care. If he wants his dog, he's probably trying to track down Lucy and Nova.'

'If they've still got it. The Semtex has a mind of his own. He may have run away from them and be roaming the streets anywhere in London.'

'Then maybe you ought to try the Battersea Dogs' Home.' It was as good a suggestion as any. If it wasn't, I didn't care. My brief flare of energy was ebbing away. There was a faint dull ache in my head, my stomach felt uneasy and . . .

'My throat is aching where your friend tried to throttle me. I can't talk any longer. Goodbye.'

Almost immediately, the phone began ringing again. It might be Martha, it might be Brendan ringing back, it might be . . .

I didn't care. Taking a leaf from Evangeline's book, I yanked the jack out of the socket and went back to bed.

CHAPTER FOURTEEN

By the time Evangeline returned, I felt a lot better—and no wonder.

'It's eleven,' I gasped, '*p.m.!* I've slept all day.'

'You needed it,' Evangeline said. 'And you're looking all the better for it.'

'But—' I was conscious of the odd feeling of dislocation you get when somehow the day has disappeared without your ever really getting a grip on it. I wanted to protest, to demand a recount, to start the day over and do better this time.

'Are you just getting back?' It wasn't Evangeline's fault that I had lost the day but, if she had been here, I might not have. 'Where have you been?'

'I had an early dinner with Nigel and we looked in at a few pubs. We ran into some of our friends. They send you best wishes and hope you're better soon.'

'Thanks.' I still felt half asleep, uncomfortable, unhappy ... there had been dreams ... bad dreams ... and then I remembered. I'd been dreaming of Sweetums. She hadn't been happy, either ... she had been furious ... trying to tell me something ... but the distance between us was too great. She hadn't been able to make me understand. That had made her madder than ever.

'You unplugged the phone again.' Evangeline pounced on the jack and shoved it back into the socket. 'No wonder I wasn't able to reach you. I thought it might be something like that.'

'Brendan called,' I said. 'He was upset because he couldn't find Dorsal. I told him what had happened. He still seemed to think we should know where Dorsal was. Not to mention the dog. The conversation became ... tedious.'

'I can imagine.' Evangeline clucked her tongue. 'We must have a word with Hi-Yi and have him do something about those Irishmen.

177

We can't have them hanging around making trouble.'

'I take it you didn't find Nova and Lucy?'

'No.' She gave a guilty start. 'What made you think I might be looking for them?'

'Come off it! I know you're not worried about Tex—'

'Out of sight, out of mind,' she murmured.

'But I also know you're not going to let Lucy and that play slip through your fingers—even though it may turn out to be just as terrible as the last one.'

'That woman has talent and good ideas. She just hasn't found her voice yet.'

'Speaking of which...' I hummed up and down the scale and swallowed experimentally a couple of times. Yes, definitely an improvement. 'I think I could use a glass of cold milk to soothe my throat a bit more.'

'You want some brandy and an egg beaten up in it, and perhaps a sprinkling of nutmeg on top. A good old-fashioned eggnog, that's the ticket for a sore throat.' She regarded me critically. 'And perhaps some arnica cream to rub on the outside for those bruises.'

'We don't have any arnica cream.'

'We'll get some tomorrow.'

'And we made eggnogs with rum in New England.' We didn't have any of that, either, and suddenly I had a craving for the sweet molasses tang of the cool thickened liquid. We ought to pick up some rum, too.

178

Evangeline had found a jug and was breaking two eggs into it. She might not be much as a cook, but she could mix a mean drink. She was mixing an awful lot of it; I realized she had talked herself into a brandy eggnog, too.

'I do believe we've underestimated Nigel,' Evangeline said. 'He really is a most personable young man and he has some very interesting ideas.'

'Evangeline!' Alarm bells began ringing. 'You haven't let him talk you into taking any financial advice from him?'

'Really, Trixie!' Evangeline gave me a withering look. 'I'm not insane!'

'Maybe not financially...' I sank back in my chair with relief.

'We have never seen Nigel at his best.' Evangeline ignored my remark. 'Not operating in a social scene with strangers.'

'*What* social scene?' My suspicions were aroused. 'Where did you take him?'

'Oh...' She poured brandy recklessly into the jug, a faraway look in her eyes. 'Here and there ... round and about...'

'You didn't find Nova and Lucy.' She'd have been cock-a-hoop if she had, but she was clearly not entirely displeased with her day. 'Did you get any clues about where they live?'

'Not directly...' She was sparing with the milk, but then emptied a small carton of cream into the jug. 'We wound up at the Queen and

Country and ran into Vic and his friends. They were there to see the full show. It seems that, after we left, what passed for the management had had to stop the show and give the audience their money back or tickets for another night. The ventilation was so poor that they couldn't clear the smoke in time for the show to continue that night.

'The boys also,' she continued thoughtfully, 'got our tickets replaced and gave them to me. We really must see the rest of that show. It wasn't too bad.'

'Uh-huh.' I felt I'd probably seen enough of *The Mist in the Meadow*—and especially the mist—to last me the rest of my life. But Evangeline was always determined to have her and everyone else's money's worth. 'And was that where you discovered how sociable Nigel could be?'

'Why, yes. He got on so well with everybody, I was very favourably impressed. Especially with that shy little Ledbetter.'

Ledbetter, the stake-holder. And Nigel, with his unerring nose for money and his sharp eye for the main chance. Alarm bells shrilled again. I wondered just how high the stakes Ledbetter held were—and how susceptible he was to flattery.

'There now—' Evangeline handed me a glass of cool creamy liquid. 'Wrap your tonsils around that. It's just what the doctor ordered.'

Well . . . maybe a doctor in the good old days

180

before the medical profession concerned itself with little matters like cholesterol and alcoholism. The days when a Victorian lady took to her couch for a decade or two with the prescribed eggnogs and/or laudanum. I sure wouldn't have to worry about getting back to sleep tonight, despite my afternoon-long nap.

But that was another thing. In a vague way, I felt as though the shadowy dreams were still there waiting to claim me again—and I could do without them. In fact...

'Evangeline?' I sniffed the air uneasily. 'Can you smell heliotrope?'

'Heaven forfend!' But she lifted her head and sniffed, too, suddenly as uneasy as I was. Her forehead creased; she looked around suspiciously.

'Nonsense!' She was speaking to herself, not to me. 'It's impossible!' She set down her glass and charged over to the far corner, returning with the wastebasket, which she upended in the middle of the kitchen floor.

'There! There's your explanation!' She pounced on the torn-up pieces of Sweetums's original letter (had it been that long since we'd emptied the wastebasket?) and waved them at me.

I stepped back, repelled and dizzied by the waves of sickly sweet scent emanating from the paper. 'Please, Evangeline—'

'The last of Sweetums Carew!' She carried them over and deposited them ceremoniously

181

in the depths of the black binliner. 'And good riddance!'

The cloying scent still hung in the air, perhaps some of it clung to the debris which had been discarded on top of it. Sweetums must have saturated her notepaper in the stuff.

'Now forget her and let's relax.' Evangeline picked up her drink and the jug and strolled through into the living room, leaving the contents of the wastebasket still in a heap on the floor.

Automatically, I shuffled everything back into the wastebasket and carried it over to the bin. Really, it was like having to clear up after Martha at the height of her childhood sloppiness. I tried to hold on to that strangely comforting thought as the scent eddied up and nearly overwhelmed me when I dumped the rest of the stuff in the bin.

Shuddering, I retreated, then braced myself and sealed off the binliner, lifted it out and took it over and placed it outside the back door by the stairs where someone would probably collect it eventually. I put a fresh liner in the bin, telling myself that the smell of heliotrope no longer lingered, however faintly. Poor Sweetums . . . how strange that she should have survived all the feuds and battles of her life, only to succumb to a fatal accident in a strange country on what was meant to be a pleasant social occasion.

Of course it was an accident. She hadn't been

182

here long enough to add to her mortal enemies. Had she?

My glass had somehow emptied itself. I picked it up and followed Evangeline into the living room for a refill. I intended to make absolutely certain of a dreamless night.

*   *   *

In the morning, all trace of my tummy upset had disappeared. The day was bright and beautiful with the sun reflecting off the surface of the Thames, little boats sailing past leaving a gentle wake of golden ripples. The view on a day like this was almost enough to reconcile one to living deep in the heart of Docklands rather than in the centre of the city. Almost.

To prove how much better I was feeling, I got dressed before joining Evangeline in the kitchen. She looked at me sourly as I entered and I recognized the symptoms. Not only had I wrong-footed her by appearing dressed and fully made-up while she was still in her dressing gown, but she had undoubtedly finished the eggnog last night. I could have told her she was mixing a lethal potion: all that egg and cream disguises the potency of the brew until it's too late.

Evangeline was royally hungover. This did not improve her disposition, always uncertain at best first thing in the morning.

I poured my coffee and stood beside the

toaster waiting for it to pop up. It seemed safer to let her choose any subject for conversation, if she wanted to converse at all.

There was a sharp snap and the toast clattered into view.

'Don't *do* that!' Evangeline jumped and gave a muffled shriek.

'I didn't do anything—it's the toaster.'

'If you're going to butter that toast, please take it into the other room. I can't stand the noise.'

'That's what I thought.'

'And just what is that supposed to mean?' Evangeline attempted to turn her head indignantly, but stopped in mid-turn and clutched it with both hands instead.

'You're sure *you* wouldn't like to go back to bed today?'

'I have always been slightly allergic to eggs,' Evangeline announced with dignity.

'Especially when you add a pint of brandy to them.' I added more coffee to her cup, not that I thought it would do much good at this stage.

'I'm glad to see you up and ready for action.' She changed the subject as though she were dressed and ready to face the day herself. 'We have been overlooking Lunchtime Theatre, I have discovered. It is time to remedy that. We are lunching today at the Scarlet Swan. I have made arrangements with Eddie.' She rose majestically to her feet and swayed for a moment before taking a bearing on the door

184

and heading for it slowly but determinedly.

'It won't take me a moment to dress.' She lied beautifully. She always did.

Nobly, I refrained from humming 'Little Brown Jug' as she exited. Besides, it wasn't a brown earthenware jug, it was a beautiful glass claret jug with a silver lid. I looked at it as I put the cups and saucers down beside it in the sink. It must be part of Ros's collection; she had been heavy on fine china and glass. I hoped she still would be when the time came to return everything—whenever that might be.

Although their situations seemed to be easing, I noticed that none of our dear friends and neighbours were rushing to retrieve their belongings. I didn't think they were motivated solely by altruistic considerations. It was more likely that they felt the bailiffs had been defeated only temporarily and might renew their offensive when they had had time to regroup. Mariah was doing her best to stem the rising tide, but she had her work cut out for her.

There was another muffled shriek from Evangeline as the telephone rang and I went to answer it.

'It's all right,' I called out. 'It's only Eddie. He's waiting downstairs with the taxi. I told him we'd be down in a few more minutes.'

'Speak for yourself!' Evangeline sailed into the living room, stately as a galleon, and trying for as little jarring movement. '*I* am

185

ready now.'

We can both do it, of course. It's a legacy from the years of quick-change performances in run-down theatres where the icy chill of the dressing rooms was as motivating as the knowledge that you were due back on stage in forty-five seconds.

'Don't just stand there.' She waved her make-up case at me; she'd put her face on in the taxi. 'Go and get the lift!'

'I'll get my handbag first.' I dived for my room and caught up my bag and coat.

She was in the foyer when I returned and the lift doors were opening. She sailed in and leaned against the opposite wall with her eyes closed, leaving me to push the button for our descent.

I knew better than to speak to her. I concentrated on ignoring her until we reached the ground floor, when she marched out ahead of me, down the steps and into the waiting taxi.

'The Scarlet Swan,' she directed.

We sat there motionless.

'If you please, Eddie,' I said sweetly.

We still sat there.

'We want to go to the Scarlet Swan pub,' Evangeline said between clenched teeth. 'We want to be there for lunch.'

'Are you sure?' Eddie asked.

'Why shouldn't we be?' I asked.

'Well, you know . . . it's a Women Only pub.'

'It may have escaped your notice, Eddie,'

Evangeline said, 'but *we* are women.'

'Yes, but—' He cast about frantically. 'It's in Battersea. It's *south* of the river.'

'Oh, good.' Evangeline tried sarcasm. 'That's just where Battersea always used to be. I'm so glad they haven't moved it.'

'But—'

'Drive!' she ordered.

'If you must.' He slipped the cab into gear. 'You'll be asking for the Drill Hall next,' he muttered.

'If they have a good show on, perhaps we will.' Evangeline opened her make-up case with a decisive snap and settled down to recreating her face, thoroughly revived by the altercation.

Eddie lapsed into a disapproving sulk and gave all his attention to the road, managing to bounce us in and out of every pothole between Docklands and the Scarlet Swan.

The first thing I saw was the large placard in the window announcing: AMAZONS IN ARMS.

'Uh-oh,' I said. 'Evangeline, do you really think—?'

'Look!' she commanded.

The second thing I saw was Tex gallumphing across the pavement to greet us as old friends.

CHAPTER FIFTEEN

I'd seen worse adaptations of *Lysistrata*, although perhaps none quite so peculiarly slanted. However, the cast was lively and enthusiastic, the acting ranged from competent to inspired and the audience entered into the spirit of the piece. Also, the performance was mercifully short, since the theory of lunchtime theatre is that jaded office workers can drop in and imbibe culture and lunch simultaneously. The theory seemed to work well; the performance had been crowded and the atmosphere friendly and relaxed, with everyone having a good time. I'd had a good time myself. I realized abruptly that this was the first show we'd seen in ages that hadn't had one or several of the men from the Open and Shut Club in its audience. It was rather refreshing.

The fact that we were recognized and treated like royalty had done nothing to lessen our enjoyment, of course, and Lucy and Nova had basked in our reflected glory. We sat at a long trestle table facing the stage and feasted on a hearty vegetable soup and freshly baked wholemeal rolls with lashings of unsalted butter while watching the performance. Tex lay beneath the table at our feet and was quite forgiving when nothing more interesting than the occasional crust was tossed to him. Tex . . .

'You really are going to have to give him back, you know.' I tried to impress the fact on Lucy after the performance.

'Oh, but he's so *happy* here with us.' Lucy tangled one hand in Tex's fur and avoided our eyes. 'Aren't you, Tex?'

'That isn't the point.' How could I get through to her? 'Tex *belongs* to somebody. His master wants him back. He's a thoroughbred dog, an *expensive* dog—'

'He sure is,' Nova muttered. 'He eats like a horse.'

'He is Dorsal Finn's dog.' I tried to keep to the point, although I felt that Nova had another good bargaining counter. 'And Dorsal is a dangerous man. He may even be crazy.' I fingered my throat. 'He's paranoid about getting Tex back. You can't just dognap somebody else's animal.'

'Animals have rights, too,' Lucy muttered.

Thump-thump-thump. The tail hit the floor beside my feet. Tex agreed with her.

'You could get in serious trouble over this,' I said severely. Evangeline nodded agreement.

Lucy pouted and bent over to rub her forehead against Tex's. 'You'd rather be with me, wouldn't you, lovey?'

Thump-thump-thump.

'It's only a matter of time'—I spoke over her head to Nova—'until Dorsal goes to the police.' I didn't add that the police were

189

unlikely to be very sympathetic towards an Irishman reporting that he'd lost his Semtex. Even when they'd sorted it out, I doubted that they'd enjoy the joke. Good enough for him, they might think.

'I've been trying to get her to see reason.' Nova sighed. 'But it's no use. She's besotted by that mutt.'

We were talking about her as though she weren't there. Lucy returned the compliment by ignoring us utterly, but she was paying attention, all right.

'Tex—' Lucy spoke over *our* heads directly to Evangeline, obviously deciding she was the most likely ally at the moment. 'Tex is my inspiration! I can work so much better when he's sitting at my feet. I've done *pages* more of *Hamlet Swoons* since I've had him.'

'Have you?' Evangeline switched sides without a moment's qualm. 'In that case, perhaps a few more days' delay in returning him wouldn't matter all that much.'

'Dorsal is dangerous,' I repeated. Evangeline hadn't had those steel fingers tightening around *her* throat.

'How much longer do you think it will take you to finish the play?' Evangeline didn't care; she just wanted that script.

'Oh, I don't know...' Lucy looked off into the distance. Lunch hour was well and truly over and the room was nearly empty, only a few stragglers or, possibly, unemployed remained.

190

'If anything happened to Tex,' Lucy declared tragically, 'I'm not sure I could ever work again.'

'Nothing will happen to Tex.' Evangeline reacted to the implied threat instantly.

'Of course it won't.' I glared at her. 'Dorsal loves that hound. He's taken very good care of it in the past, he's not going to mistreat it now. Look how healthy and strong Tex is.' *And a disgusting ingrate*, I just stopped myself from adding. All that care and affection apparently didn't work both ways.

Thump-thump-thump. He knew he was under discussion and that suited him just fine.

'Maybe you can go and visit Tex,' Nova offered, weakening her case from the start with that *maybe*. 'Maybe you can even take him for walks sometimes. We can insist on visiting privileges as a condition of giving him back.'

'No!' Lucy threw her arms around Tex's neck. 'You don't understand. None of you understand. I want him *here*. With *me*. All the time! You want to stay with Lucy, don't you, Tex?'

Thump-thump-thump.

'You see? He does! He's *my* dog now!'

'He takes up an awful lot of room, Lu,' Nova said. 'And he eats an awful lot—'

'He can have *my* share of the food! *I* don't begrudge it to him!'

'I didn't mean that. I mean—' Nova

191

brightened. 'I know! If you really want a pet, why don't we get a cat?'

'You're all against me!' Lucy surged to her feet; Tex hoisted himself up to stand beside her. He looked as though he might be considering giving a growl or two in sympathy.

'No, no,' Nova protested. 'Take it easy, Lu. We're on your side. Honestly. We'll work something out.'

'You don't *care* about Tex!'

'Well, not as much as you do, no.'

'Oh!' Lucy turned and darted away towards the dressing rooms, Tex at her heels.

'I guess I blew that one.' Nova looked after them ruefully.

'She'll be all right, won't she?' I asked anxiously. I was beginning to mistrust dog lovers. Did they all get so unbalanced about their pets, or was it just some special effect Tex had on people?

'Sure, sure. I'll give her a bit of time to cool off and then I'll go and try to talk sense to her.'

'Perhaps I should talk to her.' Evangeline stood.

'You were going to let us see those first ten pages of the script,' I reminded Nova and, incidentally, Evangeline. I didn't want Evangeline rushing off and committing herself irrevocably to that script until we had a better idea of just how good it might be.

'Oh, Lu's got a lot more done than that now,' Nova said eagerly. 'I hate to admit it, but that dog *does* seem to inspire her. That's why I haven't been rushing to get him back to the Green Colleen, the way I promised you.' She gave an apologetic bob of the head, then slid a sidelong glance at Evangeline. 'I didn't think a bit of delay would make all that much difference.'

'It nearly got me killed,' I said indignantly.

'Mmm, yes,' Evangeline said. 'But if the script is really going well...'

'Oh, it is,' Nova affirmed. 'You're going to be delighted with it. And Lu has really immersed herself in it. She's getting new ideas every minute.'

'I'd still like to see what's actually been written so far.' Mine was the lone small voice of reason. Nova and Evangeline were nodding happily at each other, lost in the haze of self-deceiving anticipation and optimism that results in so many unlikely productions opening on Wednesday nights and closing on Saturday nights.

'Dear Lucy is *so* creative,' Evangeline murmured.

'I'll say! Do you know, she's discovered that when Bernhardt's *Hamlet* opened in London, the reviewer for *Punch* said that all it needed to be perfect was Henry Irving as Ophelia! It's given Lucy a great concept. She's exploring it now. I mean, he lives right here in England now. And you've played opposite each other so many times. Perhaps you could sound him out

193

about it ...?'

'Do you mean what I think you mean?' Evangeline asked faintly. Even she was going to baulk at that idea.

'Beauregard Sylvester as Ophelia!' I was momentarily stunned. 'That's some concept, all right. I just don't want to be around when you suggest it to him.'

Then I realized I was a liar. I *did* want to be around. Preferably in a bomb shelter—but I wouldn't miss it for the world.

'I'd discourage that idea, if I were you, my dear.' Evangeline had her own agenda and Beau's sensibilities had no place on it. 'I see *Hamlet Swoons* as a vehicle for a female star only. Bringing in a male lead would dissipate the effect, weaken the impact of the Bernhardt character ... in fact, ruin the play.'

For an instant, I had a glorious vision of Ophelia picking up Hamlet by the scruff of the neck, shaking him, and hurling him across the stage when he tried to hie her to a nunnery.

'I see what you mean. I'll tell Lucy. I'm sure you're right.' Nova got the message: Evangeline wasn't going to share the limelight. With anyone. I already knew that. It was time for me to pay another visit to *Gather Ye Rosebuds* and investigate the possibility of commissioning a new musical from that clever—

There was the loud gunning of a motor outside and the scream of tortured machinery.

194

Something crashed against the building and there was a loud scraping noise. The motor gunned explosively and there was another thud.

'Oh, my God!' Nova had pinpointed the source of all the noise and leaped for the door. 'It's Lucy! She's got the taxi! And she can't drive.'

Evangeline and I raced after her, reaching the door just in time to see the taxi lurching off into the distance. A shaggy grey head protruded from the side window, yelping joyfully at all the excitement.

'If she can't drive, she won't get far,' Evangeline said.

'She seems to be doing all right so far.' I watched the taxi take the corner on two wheels and disappear from sight.

'She's only had two lessons,' Nova moaned. 'She's never been out in traffic at all. She'll kill herself.'

I listened hopefully for the sound of a crash, but only heard the throb of the motor fading away. It seemed to be running a bit more smoothly.

'She's ahead of the rush-hour traffic.' Evangeline tried to cheer Nova. 'If there aren't too many cars on the road, she should have a sporting chance.'

I thought Lucy's best chance might be if she got picked up by the cops, but tact prevailed and I didn't say so.

'Let's find a taxi.' Evangeline looked around the deserted street. 'We can get to your place ahead of her.'

'Uuuh...' Nova looked at us guiltily. I began to suspect that she did not want us to know where they lived. 'I'm not sure she's going home. I've seen her in these moods before. She runs away and hides until you give her what she wants, or she forgets it.'

'Where does she run to?' Evangeline asked.

'How long does it take until she shows up again?' I had a more pertinent question. We might not have all that much time. Unless Brendan caught up with Dorsal and got him under some sort of control. Right now, Dorsal was a wild man bound on vengeance, like some crazed gunslinger in an old Western—which might be where he got some of his ideas about horse thieves and hanging.

'I don't know.' Nova chose to answer Evangeline's question first. Maybe it was the easier one. 'She has half a dozen little hidey-holes, I think. She has some literary friends I've never met. She stays with them when it gets too hot in the kitchen.'

'Does she do this often?' We were getting an interesting sidelight on their domestic situation.

'Often enough. Lu has a real artistic temperament. The least little thing can upset her and throw her off stride.'

'And how long does it usually take her to,

um, recover her composure?'

'You never can tell. It all depends on how upset she's been. Of course,' Nova brightened, 'she's never gone running to any of her other friends with a hulking great dog in tow. That might dampen their enthusiasm for taking her in.'

'We can but hope.' I was glad to see Evangeline pull her cellphone out of her bag and begin dialling Eddie's number. We didn't want to be stuck here for the rest of the day.

'I'd better get moving—' Nova tried to get away. 'I'll go home and do some telephoning around. Lu might have gone to someone we both know. Angie has a nice big back garden. She's a definite possibility.'

'We'll give you a lift.' Evangeline caught her arm as she turned away to leave. 'And you can use my phone.' She thrust it at her.

'But—' Trapped, Nova looked around wildly. 'It's too soon to start telephoning. Lu hasn't had time to get anywhere yet. If she doesn't crash the car first.'

'In any case, we'll take you home.' Evangeline was firm. 'She may go there to leave you a note. When she stops off to pick up her script. I assume she'll continue working on it—since Tex is such an inspiration to her.'

'We may even get there before she does.' I tried to inject a note of cheer. 'If she's such a bad driver, it will take her a long time to get through all the mid-town traffic.'

197

'If she doesn't kill herself first.' Nova slumped, dejected. She knew when she was beaten and we could get her home a lot faster than public transport could.

Eddie must have been tootling about not very far away, perhaps waiting for our call. He regarded Nova with disapproval, but said nothing, not even when she gave him the address. The expression on his face was enough.

We drove in silence all the long winding way, each lost in her own thoughts. Nova began to shift restlessly as we moved into a gloomy district dominated by shabby tower blocks defaced by graffiti and surrounded by piles of litter and debris.

'Thanks for the lift.' She made a last-ditch attempt to escape the inevitable, yanking the door open as the taxi drew up to the kerb. 'Very kind of you. I'll let you know about Lu—'

'Nonsense, my dear.' Evangeline was on her heels. 'We'll see you inside. There may be something we can do.'

'That's right.' I wasn't going to miss this, either. 'Three heads are better than one.'

'I'll wait.' Eddie turned off the engine and slumped down in the front seat, bracing himself for the worst. 'Unless you want me to come in with you?'

'No!' Nova almost shouted.

'That won't be necessary, thank you, Eddie,' Evangeline said graciously. 'We may not be long.'

That was obviously the first cheering bit of news Nova had heard all afternoon. There was a spring in her step as she led us up the path of one in a row of terraced houses directly opposite the housing estate. It must have been a fairly pleasant area once, before the tower blocks had gone up.

'Hell!' Nova had been fumbling in the pocket of her jeans, now she remembered. 'Lucy's taken my keys. I'll have to go in through the window. Don't worry, once we're inside, we're all right. You stay here,' she added, just in case we had any idea of following her through the window. 'Old Mrs Ames knows me. You might frighten her.'

She looked over her shoulder at the looming tower blocks before she began rapping on the window and calling out: 'It's only me, Mrs Ames. I'm locked out again. Just coming through.' She raised the window and looked over her shoulder again.

'Just crowd up close,' she directed Evangeline and me, 'so no one can see what we're doing. I wouldn't want anyone to get the idea it's easy to get into this place.' She ducked down as we obeyed and hurled herself through the opening.

I caught a glimpse of white hair and wild staring eyes as the curtains flew inwards with the rush of Nova's passage.

'I'll be right with you.' Nova's head popped

up as she closed the window and disappeared.

A moment later, the front door opened. 'We're upstairs,' Nova said, leading the way up a flight of steep and narrow stairs. The railing was wobbly and there were loose floorboards in the tiny hallway just outside the door of the flat. Nova stooped and lifted one of the floorboards, pulling out a spare key. She turned the key in the lock and swung open the door. 'Come in.'

I'm not sure what I had expected, but we walked into a pleasant little sitting room, which might have been reasonably tidy were it not for a large rubber ball, a couple of well-gnawed bones, and a rumpled corner of the rug turned back and looking as if it too had been gnawed. There was also a scattering of torn newspapers and magazines across the floor.

'She's not back yet,' Nova reported, having taken a quick look into a couple of rooms opening off the sitting room. 'If she's coming back. I hope she's all right. I haven't even taught her how to reverse yet. She can only go forward and she can never remember to signal for a turn.'

Neither could half the driving population, from what I had seen. They glared at you and switched on their indicator light only when they had braked six inches away from your knee. It was all your fault for not being a mind-reader and knowing they were going to turn down that street.

200

'Lucy is very clever. She'll manage beautifully.' Evangeline spoke absently. She had spotted the desk in the corner of the room and all her attention was concentrated on that. A half-written page sat enticingly in an old manual typewriter, a small stack of typed pages rested beside it. Evangeline sidled closer.

'That bloody dog was in the front seat with her.' Nova chewed at a fingernail. 'If he starts jumping around, she could lose control, not that she has much control in the first place.'

I was more worried about Evangeline's control. She was beside the desk now, trying to look as though she wasn't craning her neck for all she was worth. Her fingers were twitching.

'Evangeline...' I said warningly.

'Yes?' She gave me an innocent wide-eyed stare, then turned to Nova. 'I'm afraid I'm getting a headache, my dear. Could you possibly get me a glass of water so that I can take my aspirin?'

'Sure. Would you like anything else? A cup of tea or coffee? A glass of sherry?'

'Just a glass of water.' Evangeline gave a martyr's smile. 'Please.'

'Right away!' Nova dashed through one of the doorways and we heard glasses rattling.

Evangeline was already bending over the typewriter, shamelessly devouring the typed words. 'Oh, yes,' she said enthusiastically. 'Oh, yes!'

'Evangeline, get away from there! She'll be

201

back in a second.'

'Yes.' Evangeline straightened and looked at me unseeingly. 'Do I hear a car outside? Has Lucy come back? Or—Trixie! Eddie is still out there, isn't he? He's still waiting for us?'

I dashed for the window to check. All we needed was to be abandoned here with Nova, and without transport back to civilization.

'He's still there,' I reported thankfully. 'He's sitting there reading a newspaper.'

'Oh, good.' She sounded too smug. I turned back to her suspiciously, but the page was still in the typewriter and the desk seemed as it had been before.

'Here you are.' Nova returned bearing a tumbler of water.

'Thank you so much.' Evangeline took the glass and fumbled two aspirins awkwardly into her mouth, swallowing with a grimace.

'All right?' Nova watched her anxiously.

'Actually, my dear, I'm afraid not.' Evangeline did another martyred but brave smile. 'It's worse, much worse. I *did* so want to stay here with you and wait for Lucy but ... my head ...' She brushed the back of one hand across her forehead. I caught a dangerous flash of her eyes from under the lowered lids.

'I'd better get her home.' I moved forward, responding to my cue. 'Before it really closes in on her.'

'While I can still walk.' Evangeline swayed dramatically in the direction of the door. 'I

202

think I can still manage the stairs ... just.'

'You'd better,' I said. 'We're not going to carry you.'

Nova hovered anxiously while Evangeline swayed down the narrow staircase. Eddie took one look at the apparition heading towards him and leaped to open the cab door.

'I'll let you know as soon as I hear from Lucy,' Nova said.

'Please do.' Evangeline lay back against the seat and closed her eyes.

I perched on the edge of the seat and tried to keep the jaundiced expression off my face—at least until no one was watching. Evangeline opened her eyes, took one look at me, and shut them again. 'Home, home, Eddie, quickly,' she murmured piteously.

Eddie gunned the motor and we shot away from the kerb as though jet-propelled. Evangeline winced. I noticed that she was holding one arm awkwardly and wondered if she had knocked it when stumbling dramatically down the stairs. That would teach her to overact.

CHAPTER SIXTEEN

With very little effort, I could work up a real hatred for the telephone. It began ringing as soon as we walked into the living room.

'Don't answer!' Evangeline glared at the phone. 'I can't think of one single person we really want to talk to, can you?'

'Martha.' I headed for the phone. 'Or one of the children.'

Evangeline snorted, but waited to find out who it was. That was her mistake. As I lifted the receiver, I saw two inches of crisp white cuff slip from the sleeve of her coat. It took me only a moment to realize that she wasn't wearing a blouse with white cuffs. I set down the phone unanswered and advanced on her.

'I think I'll go to my room.' She backed away uneasily.

'Not yet, you won't.' I caught her arm. 'Not until I see what you've got up your sleeve.'

'Nothing.' But there was a sharp crackle of paper beneath my fingertips. 'Let me go!'

'You stole Lucy's play!' Suddenly the reason for her desire for a glass of water, her urgency that I make sure Eddie was still waiting outside, became clear. While our backs were turned, she had helped herself from the desk.

'It's *my* play!' Now that she was caught, she shrugged calmly out of her coat and retrieved the script from the sleeve. 'I had to leave the page on top of the pile beside the typewriter, unfortunately, and I didn't quite dare to take the page from the machine in case Nova noticed. But I've memorized them. If I can get to pen and paper quickly enough, I should be able to write them down verbatim.'

204

'You stole it,' I repeated. 'How could you? Have you no shame? No shame at all?'

Of course, she hadn't. She was quite pleased with herself, in fact. Humming softly, she settled herself in an armchair and began riffling through the pages.

'You call Eddie back this minute and send him over to return that play!'

'Do you really think he'd go? He didn't like that neighbourhood in broad daylight and it's beginning to get dark now.'

'You've got to return it!' I seemed to have been uttering variations of that remark all day.

'*You* can return it, if you're so concerned about it,' Evangeline said serenely. 'After I photocopy it.'

'Evangeline!'

'Zis role ees a shallenge sush as I 'ave nevair faced before! Zis role could be zee culmination of my career.'

'No, Evangeline!' She was hopeless. 'Not with that phoney French accent.'

'But—' She looked puzzled. 'It's written in that accent.'

I might have known it! 'Let me see that!' I snatched for the script, but she held it out of reach.

'I'm going to read it first! It's *my* play! Any minor problems with it can be ironed out when we talk to Lucy.'

'*If* we talk to Lucy. By now, she may be on her way to a croft in the wilds of Scotland—just

205

so she can hang on to that damned dog.'

'The artistic temperament,' Evangeline murmured. 'How well we know it.'

The telephone rang again. I should have pulled the jack out.

'It might be Nova,' Evangeline said. 'Lucy may be back.'

'Yeah, and she may have found her play missing!' The phone continued to ring. Neither of us moved to answer it.

'You get it,' Evangeline directed. 'I'll go and write down as much as I can remember from the pages I had to leave behind. Then, at least, we'll have something to work with.' She disappeared into her bedroom.

'Hello?' I was going to make short shrift of this call and then disconnect the phone for the rest of the night.

'Hello ... Trixie? Is that Trixie Dolan?' The male voice was vaguely familiar, but not immediately identifiable.

'Yes ...' I admitted cautiously. At least, he didn't have an Irish accent. 'Who is this?'

'Oh, sorry. It's Greg. From the Open and Shut Club.'

'Oh, yes.'

'I'm sorry, I hope I'm not disturbing you.' I guess I didn't sound exactly welcoming. 'I was just—*We* were wondering if you were all right? You and Miss Sinclair?'

'We're just fine. Why shouldn't we be?'

'But you're not here. At the Wounded Lion.

206

It's Opening Night for *Give No Quarter*. We were worried ... concerned ...'

'We went to a lunchtime matinée today at the Scarlet Swan. Even for us, one show a day is enough.'

'Of course, of course. I'm glad there's nothing wrong. Perhaps you'll be coming along tomorrow night? I think you'd find it very interesting. It's a play, but with incidental music. Some of it sounds quite good.'

'Oh?' I have to admit it, he'd hooked me. There was so little in the musical line on offer that even incidental music was worth looking into. 'Perhaps we could make it tomorrow night.'

'Good. Tell you what, why don't we all meet here and the club will take you to dinner? Then we can all see the show together. It isn't the same without you.'

'No dinner,' I said firmly. I'd had enough pub meals to last me a long time, even though today's lunch had been pretty good. Come to think of it, I was getting a bit fed up with the Open and Shutters, too. *Why* wasn't it the same without us? They'd managed happily before we appeared on the scene. It wasn't as though we were their girlfriends. And that was another thing: where were their girlfriends? They were a group of good-looking, healthy, solvent young men not obviously overly devoted to each other, so where were the young women they should have by their sides?

'Trixie ...?' He had been waiting for me to say something more; in my preoccupation, I had let the silence go on too long. 'Are you still there?'

'Yes, I was just thinking...'

'Changing your mind, I hope. The food is really quite good at the Wounded Lion.'

'We already have a dinner date.' It seemed the easiest way out. 'We might look in on the show later—and we'll be bringing our guests.'

'The Sylvesters? How smashing!' His enthusiasm would have put him on Evangeline's black list instantly.

'Not them.' I had actually been thinking of introducing Ros to the group. She was such a nice, pretty young woman and she could use some cheering up. 'We *do* have other friends.'

'Of course, of course. I didn't mean to imply—'

'I'm glad to hear that.' I'd had just about enough of Greg. 'And now, if you'll excuse me, there's someone at the door.' The doorbell rang as I spoke, making an honest woman of me.

'Yes, yes, I hear it. We'll see you tomorrow night, then.'

'Don't bet on it.' But he had already hung up.

I crossed to answer the doorbell, aware that Evangeline always as curious as a cat—was hovering in her bedroom doorway to see who it was.

208

'Come in, Nigel.' I hoped she was disappointed.

'Nigel, dear, what a coincidence!' Evangeline swooped forward. 'I was just about to ring you.'

'Ah! Good!' A bit surer of his welcome, Nigel stepped into the living room, looking at her expectantly. 'Why?'

'No, no, you first.' Evangeline was consumed with inquisitiveness. 'After all, if it was important enough for you to come up here...' She made it sound as though he had trekked to the North Pole, and she had quite lost sight of the fact that he was saving the cost of a telephone call by that short hop in the lift. She tended to forget that other people might need to economize. Especially those without jobs.

'Ah! Well! Not all that important, perhaps. Just a little invitation. I've heard there's a new show opening at the Wounded Lion and thought you might like to be my guests. Perhaps have a meal there, too. Tomorrow night? Or any evening you like.'

'That's *Give No Quarter*, right?' Either this was going to be the most popular show in town, or it was the cheapest.

'Ah, right! You've heard about it, then?' He beamed at me, as though his taste in entertainment had been confirmed.

'It has incidental music,' I said. 'Where did you hear about it, Nigel?' He had never struck

209

me as being particularly knowledgeable about the fringe theatre—or even the West End.

'Oh! Ah! One of the chappies you introduced me to the other night.' He looked at Evangeline. 'Thought I might like to know about it and rang me.'

'I noticed you were getting along awfully well with Ledbetter.'

'Ledbetter, yes. That's the one. Jolly clever of you to know straightaway.' He beamed at her.

'Elementary, my dear Nigel.' She beamed back.

Maybe, but that was the easiest question of the lot. A more pertinent one was just why the Open and Shut Club were so determined to get us to the Wounded Lion. Was the show really that good? Was our company so desirable? Or did they have a bet riding on whether Greg or Nigel was the more persuasive? Certainly, they had mounted a determined two-pronged attack to ensure our presence tomorrow night. Some sort of surprise party? But it wasn't the birthday of either of us, nor any anniversary that I could recall.

'I'll collect you about seven tomorrow night, shall I? That will give us time to have dinner there before the show.'

'Oh, no, not dinner,' I said. All roads might lead to the Wounded Lion, but I certainly wasn't going to eat there. Nigel looked so disappointed I figured Ledbetter was actually going to pay for the meal.

'Come up here about six-thirty,' I said. 'We'll eat here before we go.' Our microwave oven was as good as any pub's microwave.

'Ah! If you're sure? Not too much trouble?' Nigel's face cleared; he didn't mind where he ate as long as he wasn't paying for it.

'We insist,' I assured him.

*   *   *

The Wounded Lion was a lot more upmarket than most of the pubs we had visited lately, with the possible exception of the Happy Larry. There were window boxes filled with flowers and greenery, carriage lamps flanking the doors, mullioned windows and a long deep balcony overhanging the entrance and running along the length of the building.

'Very picturesque.' Evangeline took it all in and nodded approval. 'Just like a backdrop for a movie.'

'It *is* very old,' Nigel said. 'Ah ... eighteenth ... seventeenth ... sixteenth ...' He groped for a suitable century.

'Not as old as you might think,' a voice said behind us. 'One of the last coaching inns, true, but a replacement for a much earlier inn on the same site. Now that one was really old, built by a returned Crusader. Hence the name. Some legends say it refers to Coeur de Lion, others that the Crusader actually encountered a

211

wounded lion in the desert.'

'Terence!' We whirled to face him. 'What a surprise!'

'What are *you* doing here?' Evangeline sounded more annoyed than surprised.

'I've heard the show is excellent; I wanted to catch it before it transfers to the West End.' Yet Terence looked obscurely guilty, as though expecting to be accused of something reprehensible. Disloyalty, perhaps, or even dancing on a grave. 'I hope you don't think it's too disrespectful, but I don't think Sweetums would have minded.'

'I'm sure she wouldn't,' I said quickly and, I hope, loudly enough to cover Evangeline's snort. 'She wouldn't want you to mourn.' I sent Evangeline a dirty look.

'That's what I thought. She had a long and productive career and we are rich in the legacy she left us.' He pushed open the door and we entered the cheery saloon bar.

Engraved mirrors behind the long bar reflected groups of laughing customers and the many small tables, each with its own carriage lamp and tiny vase of spring flowers. There was a piano in one corner rattling out a honky-tonk medley of music hall tunes. I realized with surprise that Vic was the pianist.

'Let me get you a drink—' Terence began.

'All taken care of, old man.' Greg appeared with large brandy snifters nearly a third full of golden liquid. Shades of Sweetums! *Were* they trying to get us drunk?

Evangeline appeared to have no such qualm as she accepted her glass.

'We're over here.' Greg led us to a table by the piano. 'Adam, get the gents a couple of drinks, will you?' he ordered carelessly.

'So glad you could make it.' Ledbetter's smile seemed a bit strained as he included Terence and Nigel. I got the idea that he would have been happier if we had come by ourselves. It was too bad Ros had had a previous engagement, she might have had a better effect on him. Or would she and Adam be a better match? Or perhaps Vic? I realized that long years of trying to pair off Martha had left a lasting automatic reaction in me. I could no longer look at an eligible bachelor without plotting the loss of his freedom.

'Any requests?' Vic called out merrily, swinging into 'No More Sugar for Daddy' with an inviting wink at me. A spattering of applause from adjoining tables egged me on.

Well, I had to stand up and sing a chorus or two, didn't I? Never mind Evangeline scowling into her snifter. Was it my fault that she couldn't carry a tune?

The applause had drowned out the warning bell, which was eventually heard to be ringing violently. So I was in a very good mood when we went upstairs to the theatre. It was obviously a fully fledged tourist trap, with a proper stage and curtain and individual

213

comfortable seats. Too bad about the play.

Historical dramas were never my strong point and Evangeline has abjured wimples ever since that made-for-TV movie *Crisis in the Convent*, which had set television back at least thirty years, not to mention what it did to religion.

The incidental music was pleasant, but not so much memorable as reminiscent. I seemed to have heard it all before. Often. And a lot better done. Unless the second act improved dramatically, there was nothing here for us.

'Coming downstairs for a drink?' Finally, the lights had gone up, the last plangent chords of the lute hovered in the air. Greg was at our elbows, trying to chivvy us into action when I, for one, just wanted to sit still, read my programme and wait for the second act to begin.

'I think not.' Evangeline was not disposed to move, either.

'Come out on the balcony then and get a breath of air,' Greg urged solicitously. 'I'll bring drinks up to you.'

Some of the audience were already crowding out on to the balcony, pulling packets of cigarettes from handbags and pockets as they went through the door. There was going to be more smoke than air on that balcony during the interval.

'Perhaps after the show,' I said. 'I want to check the programme before the next act.'

'I'll get their drinks.' Nigel jumped to his feet. 'Same again?' He was gone before we could answer.

'I'm glad to have this chance to talk to you.' Terence also remained in his seat. 'I was afraid I wasn't going to have time before I left.'

'Oh? Are you going somewhere?' I heard Evangeline ask without any particular interest as I concentrated on my programme notes. It appeared that the author was now working on a docudrama of the Irish Potato Famine with incidental music based on old Gaelic folk songs. Definitely, nothing for us here.

'Yes, quite unexpectedly. I had no plans to, but ...' Terence shrugged, looking both proud and uncomfortable. 'But I couldn't refuse, the way her family put it. I'll have to arrange for the memorial service when I get back. This is more important.'

'I'm sure Sweetums would understand,' I said automatically; the man seemed to require constant reassurance.

'Oh, I know Sweetums wouldn't mind this,' he said. 'It's not as though I were deserting her. She's coming with me—rather, I'm going with her.'

'What?' Now he had my undivided attention.

'Her family asked me to escort her— her'—he could not bring himself to say 'body'—'back to Los Angeles. When I telephoned them with my condolences and to

215

tell them that she had been happy and having a good time right up to the—the end. I thought at first that they meant for me to have her cremated and bring them the ashes, but no. Her daughter-in-law said they want to see the … body … for themselves, so they could be sure she was really dead. They wouldn't be able to believe it otherwise.'

That figured. After what Sweetums had put them through, they would probably bury her at a crossroads with a stake through her heart, just to make sure she'd never bother them again.

'I've been seeing to the arrangements,' he went on. 'We should be flying out two days after tomorrow. I … I feel it's a great honour. And the family have invited me to stay at their home and attend the funeral. I'll be representing the Magnificent Stars of Yesteryear Fan Club, of course.'

Nigel returned with our drinks and we reached for them with unseemly haste. Trust Sweetums to get herself an attractive male escort right up to the Pearly Gates.

For once, I was happy to hear the second-act bell. I didn't feel my conversational powers were adequate to any more discussion with Terence—and I was darned sure Evangeline's weren't.

By the time the show ended, we had all regained our composure. Four curtain calls seemed a bit excessive, but I joined in the

216

applause willingly. It gave us an excuse to remain in our seats while the more impatient of the audience crowded the aisles.

'You'd think they still played "God Save the Queen",' Evangeline grumbled under her breath. 'Time was when you could be trampled to death in the rush of people trying to get out before that started and they had to stand to attention until it finished. Of course, it was "the King" in those days.'

'The rush seems to be over now,' I said, as the curtains swished shut with an air of finality. 'I think it's safe to leave.'

I spoke too soon, however. There was a crush on the long balcony outside. It seemed as though some of the early birds had gone down to the bar and come back up here with their drinks. We were jostled unthinkingly as we tried to make our way to the outside stairs leading down to the courtyard.

'Over here.' Nigel shouldered through the crowd, clearing a passage for us over to the outside railing, where we paused for a moment, looking down on the cobblestoned courtyard below. It was deserted at the moment, with everyone still clustered at the bar or up here on the balcony.

More than ever, it resembled a set, waiting for the director to call: 'Action!' Light from the carriage lamps mingled with the light shining out from inside the inn to make strange wells and shadows on the rough cobblestones. I leaned over the railing, looking down, enjoying the scene and the faint scent of flowers and herbs wafting upwards from the window boxes.

And then it happened. Some rowdy gang of late leavers shoved and jostled their way past us towards the stairs.

One moment, I was just bending out over the railing slightly. The next moment, I was flying through air.

CHAPTER SEVENTEEN

Relax, I tried to tell myself on the way down.

Fall loose. It's only a one-storey drop. You've done that before in your time—and without a double.

But the time was out of joint. I seemed to be falling in slow motion. There would be no camouflaged mattresses below to soften the landing. If I hit those hard unyielding cobblestones at the wrong angle...

I felt myself tensing and tried to fight it. *Relax*...

A long piercing scream I recognized as Evangeline's ripped through the air, along with male shouts, cries and the pounding of feet along the wooden balcony.

'Oooof!' There *was* a large horsehair mattress there, after all. I was draped over it

218

and clung to it, winded.

'Woooof!' A deep echo endorsed my sentiments and the hairy mattress sagged and wobbled.

I tried to push myself upright, but slid and pitched forward, clutching my mattress around its massive neck. On the second try, I managed to sit up and discovered I was astride Tex—just like the cowboy heroes who leaped off balconies on to the backs of their faithful horses waiting below. Well, Tex *was* the size of a small pony.

'Trixie! Are you all right?' Evangeline was at my side, looking more distraught than I had ever seen her. Nigel, Terence and the members of the club were right behind her, clustering around me. 'What happened?'

'Aaarrffrruuff!' Tex decided this was a great new game and began to prance about with me still on his back.

'Stop it! Stand still!' I tugged at his ears. 'Get me off of here,' I appealed to someone, anyone.

'SIT!' Evangeline thundered in response to my plea. 'Sit! Sit!' As usual, one word from her and Tex did as he pleased. To my anguish, he decided that taking me for a canter around the courtyard would add to the fun. He set off briskly. I clung on, trying to keep my feet from dragging on the cobblestones.

'SIT!' Evangeline was still in there trying. Nigel broke away from the others and circled, trying to cut us off at the pass.

219

He had the right idea. If Tex got out of this courtyard and began roaming the streets, there was no telling where we might wind up. If only he'd stand still, I could get off.

Dizzy and disoriented, I closed my eyes, rested my head against the back of Tex's neck and held on for dear life. Maybe this was a nightmare and I would wake up soon.

'You terrible woman!' An avenging fury pushed her way through the onlookers. 'Get off that poor defenceless dog!'

'I'm trying,' I whimpered. 'I'm trying.'

With a yelp of delight, Tex whirled abruptly to carry me up to Lucy, who aimed a blow at my head. Thanks a lot, Tex.

Tex backed away, perhaps sensing that he had made a gaffe.

'Whoa! Stop!' I tried again. 'Good dog, good boy. The game is over. Stop it now and sit.'

For an indecisive moment, it seemed that he might obey.

'THE SEMTEX!' A new voice bellowed above the fray. 'To me, The Semtex!'

Amidst screams and shouts, the courtyard emptied rapidly.

'Tex!' Lucy shrieked. 'Come here, Tex.'

Tex shimmied uncertainly, looking from one to the other, then dashed to the far end of the courtyard. Only a few diehards followed him.

'Sit!' Evangeline led them, still locked in a battle of wills with the dog.

220

'Don't you dare give my dog orders, you rotten thief!' Lucy snarled.

'Lu, take it easy, Lu.' Nova was behind her now, anxiously placating.

'So you've found her out, too,' Dorsal said. 'They can't hide their true colours long. Thieves! They ought to be—'

'Dorsal, Dorsal, man. Don't be going wild.' Brendan appeared at his friend's elbow. 'You've found The Semtex. Leave it at that.' He grappled with Dorsal suddenly, forcing him back against the wall, still making soothing noises.

Tex was just bright enough to realize that he was in trouble. He backed into a corner, cringing lower to the ground.

Evangeline made an imperious gesture and Terence and Nigel stepped forward quickly and lifted me off Tex's back and on to firm ground. Tex whined and licked my hand; was the party over so soon?

'You ought to know better!' Lucy raged at me. 'You could have broken his back! What do you think he is, a horse?'

'You could have fooled me,' I muttered, keeping a firm grip on both Terence and Nigel. Nigel patted my hand. Evangeline was right, we had been underestimating the dear boy.

'Are you all right?' Evangeline looked at me anxiously. 'Is anything broken? Can you walk?'

Hearing her voice at a calmer level, Tex

decided to recognize her as another old pal. He heaved himself up to greet her, his forepaws descending on her shoulders with some force.

'Down!' Evangeline was equal to the occasion; she reinforced her command with a brisk knee to his midriff. He dropped back to all fours with a startled yip.

'You kicked him!' Lucy said. 'You kicked Tex!'

'Nonsense!' Evangeline said. 'I merely reminded him of his manners.'

'Manners!' Lucy gave a short incredulous laugh. 'Nova invited you into our flat and you stole my script right off my desk—and you talk about manners!'

'Thieves!' Dorsal had broken free of Brendan. 'That's what they are! Your script and my dog. They ought to be—'

'Oh, go hang yourself!' Evangeline's patience snapped. 'You and your phone calls and threats. You should talk!'

'Now then,' Brendan said. 'Now then, let's not get excited. Why don't we go into the pub and have a drink?'

'Because I don't drink with thieves!' Dorsal said.

'That's right!' Lucy drew herself up. 'I want my script back—and, after this, I wouldn't let you play the lead if you were the last actress in the world!'

'Lu!' Nova was appalled. 'You wrote it for her! She was the only actress you visualized in

222

the role all along.'

'That was before she stole from me! Now I've changed my mind.'

'You ought to get the law on her,' Dorsal said. 'That's burglary, that is. You ought to make her pay for it.'

'Now then, now then.' Brendan tried again. 'Let's keep calm. Let's not blow this up out of all proportion. The lady will get her script back and you've got your dog back, so let's all go home and forget about it.'

He took Tex by the collar and gave a tug. Tex didn't move.

'I beg your pardon,' Lucy said, 'but that is *my* dog!'

'The devil you say!' Dorsal scowled at her. 'I'm surrounded by thieves—and now maniacs. 'Tis my dog, I've had from a pup.'

'That's all very well.' Lucy stood her ground. 'But he's mine now!'

'Be calm, Dorsal, be calm,' Brendan pleaded. 'We can work this out. We'll sit down over a pint and discuss—'

'There's nothing to discuss!' Dorsal whirled and stalked away, barking over his shoulder, 'The Semtex, heel!'

'Come here, Tex,' Lucy called sweetly.

Tex lowered himself to the ground, sank his chin into a hollow between two cobblestones, closed his eyes and whined.

'Will you look at that now?' Brendan exclaimed. He shook his head and moved

223

closer to Evangeline and me. 'No good will come of this,' he brooded. 'No good at all.'

'This is your last chance, you dirty ingrate!' Dorsal advanced on Tex threateningly. 'Come here at once!'

'Come to me, Tex,' Lucy crooned. 'Come to your Lucy-Lu.'

'HERE, THE SEMTEX!'

'Come to Lucy, darling Tex...'

Reluctantly, Tex inched forward on his belly, avoiding eye contact with Dorsal, until his head rested on Lucy's feet. He shuddered and closed his eyes again.

'You see?' Lucy was triumphant. 'He's chosen me. He wants to be with me. He's *my* dog now!'

I wanted to close my eyes, too. I can't stand bloodshed. I felt Evangeline's hand close on my arm as she pulled me into the shadows and we began backing towards the way out.

'Tex is coming home with me,' Lucy said.

'Oh, the black look on his face,' Brendan moaned. 'Oh, the killing fury of that look. There's death in the air tonight!'

'Will ye stop keening like an old woman!' Dorsal turned on him, fists clenched.

Nigel bumped into us as he backed away, too.

'Be calm, Dorsal, calm,' Brendan said.

'Please step aside.' Lucy was not going to hesitate to rub salt in a wound. 'We're ready to leave now.'

'All right! All right!' Dorsal turned to her, his face thunderous. He hitched up his belt. 'All right, no one can say I'm not a reasonable man. So, do I move in with you? Or do you move in with me?'

'Now wait just a minute,' Nova protested. 'Lucy lives with me!'

'And what about our flat-share, Dorsal?' Brendan bleated.

'All right!' Dorsal nodded decisively. 'We'll need a bigger place then.'

We had reached the courtyard exit. We turned and ran.

*　　*　　*

'Lucy will come round,' Evangeline said in the morning.

'Don't be too sure.' I was only half listening; I had my own problem. 'Stealing the only copy of a script is pretty unforgivable.'

'I'll guarantee it.' Evangeline glanced at her watch complacently. 'I've ordered flowers to be delivered to her at ten o'clock, champagne at noon, chocolates at three, a hamper of teatime goodies at five, more flowers at seven, and a bottle of brandy and Benedictine at nine. How does that sound?'

'It's a start,' I said, but I had to admit that when Evangeline tried to make amends, she didn't do it by halves. And she was clever, not to say sneaky, about it. The spread of deliveries would ensure that Nova was present for some, if not all. And Nova was already on her side.

'There's just one little glitch,' I pointed out. 'I didn't hear any mention of the script being delivered. Or are you wrapping one page around each of the presents?'

'Ah, yes.' She took on that dreamy look I have learned to know and suspect. 'I thought that, if Lucy hasn't contacted us by tomorrow morning, you could ring Nova and invite them to lunch at the Ivy. Tell them we'll return the script then.'

'Less of that *we*, please. You got yourself into this. It's your theft—and *your* role.'

'Envy does not become you, Trixie. You must learn to rise above it. Besides, Lucy still has a great deal of work to do on the script. She can write in something for you. Perhaps a cameo appearance as the Princess of Wales coming backstage, so overwhelmed by my magnificent performance that she must congratulate me, even though she is aware that her husband and I—'

'Evangeline,' I said. 'I was pushed.'

'Don't apologize. I understand. We are all pushed, often to the limits of our endurance. It is part of the artistic—'

'Off the balcony. Last night. Deliberately.'

'What?' I had her attention now. 'Are you sure?'

'I woke up in the night remembering...' I had not gone back to sleep until dawn. 'It was a

226

delayed reaction.'

'You're sure it wasn't a false memory?' Evangeline seemed to consider that a soothing idea. 'With all those rowdy louts, pushing and shoving their way past us...'

'It wasn't an ordinary push. It was an up-and-over lift.'

'And you've just seen fit to mention it?' Evangeline's disbelief was worthy of Superintendent Heyhoe.

'I told you this was a delayed reaction. It happened so fast—and so much else kept happening—that I only registered it subconsciously. It came back to me and woke me up in the middle of the night.' I closed my eyes, then opened them quickly. It was going to take a long time before I lost that feeling of falling helplessly through the air, waiting to crash into the cobblestones.

'Why should anyone push you like that?' Evangeline asked the question I had been asking myself all night. 'Who would want to kill you?'

'*Why* would anybody want to kill me? I'm a fairly inoffensive person.' Unlike some I could mention. Evangeline had made a few new enemies recently, but Dorsal and Lucy had both been on the ground below when it happened. Hadn't they? And surely either one of them would have pushed Evangeline and not me.

'You were being very silly and leaning way

out over that railing,' Evangeline said severely. 'Perhaps someone just wanted to frighten you, to teach you a lesson, and it went too far.'

'It sure did. No'—the scene replayed itself in my mind—'no, it wasn't somebody just fooling around. Whoever did that wasn't fooling. If it hadn't been for Tex . . .'

'It probably wouldn't have killed you,' Evangeline decided briskly. 'It wasn't really all that far to fall.'

'It wouldn't have done me any good.'

The telephone rang and I glanced in its direction without enthusiasm.

'That may be dear Lucy.' Evangeline hurried to answer. 'I knew she wouldn't stay angry long.'

'The noontime champagne must just have been delivered.' It hadn't taken Lucy long to capitulate. I hoped Evangeline wouldn't decide she could cancel the rest of the deliveries.

'Hello? Oh!' Her smile faded. 'Vic, how nice—Yes. Yes, she's fine. She's right here—Oh!' She held out the phone. 'He wants to talk to you.'

'Hello, Vic.' I took it resignedly, not sure whether I wanted to talk to him. I was beginning to feel I'd had rather enough of Vic and his group of chummy gamblers.

'You're all right? You promise me you're all right? You're not suffering any—' The anxious voice wavered and broke. 'Any after effects?'

'Only a fresh collection of bruises.' I wasn't

228

sure how many. I'd find out when I showered, but I was putting off the evil moment as long as I could.

'I can't understand what happened. Did that mad Irishman get at you again? That's the second time! He's dangerous. He ought to be locked up before he can do any real damage.'

'He should be all right now that he's got his dog back. Or, at least, knows where it is.' Any future threats should be aimed at Lucy now—and she struck me as a young woman who could take care of herself.

'Are you coming to the Happy Larry tonight?' He changed the subject with evident relief. 'They're launching a revised version of *Gather Ye Rosebuds*. Lots of changes: they've added some new songs and sketches, and dropped some of the ones that didn't go over so well. It's a much stronger bet for a West End transfer now. And—' He hesitated delicately. 'And you never *did* see the second act, did you?'

'Circumstances intervened,' I agreed drily. Suddenly, the picture of Sweetums's broken body flashed across my mind. Sweetums had gone flying through the air, too, but she hadn't been as lucky as me.

'Then why don't you meet us there tonight? Bring the Sylvesters; I'm sure they'd like to see the rest of the show, too. Come early and let us stand you dinner.'

'Not tonight.' I was adamant. 'You and your friends go ahead. We might catch up with the

229

show later in the week.' When we could see it by ourselves and have a chance to talk to the writers with some privacy.

'Any night you like,' he insisted cheerfully. 'Shall we say tomorrow? Day after tomorrow?'

I had no intention of saying. I remained silent until he began to get the idea.

'Well,' he said uneasily, 'just let us know the night and we'll make the arrangements.'

'We may not be able to make it until next week,' I said. 'Or the week after. There's no hurry, is there?'

'It might close,' he said worriedly. 'Greg says he's heard something about it moving to a suburban theatre while they polish it up and work on more changes.'

'What do you mean, no hurry?' Evangeline demanded indignantly. 'We only have one more week to find a play before Cecile's show opens in Brighton.'

I waved her to silence, although not without noticing that she no longer seemed so certain that Lucy would change her mind about *Hamlet Swoons*. It seemed we were both back in the market for a starring vehicle.

Vic was still bleating on, trying to pin me down to a firm pledge that we would not move without him and his friends. I was finding his persistence increasingly irritating. Since when had we been going steady?

'We'll let you know,' I said, crossing my fingers. 'We have far too many other commitments today to even think about it, so I'll say goodbye.' I hung up while he was still bleating.

'Quite right,' Evangeline said. 'And the first thing we've got to do is get to a photocopying machine.'

CHAPTER EIGHTEEN

'You *did* tell Lucy one o'clock, didn't you?' Evangeline smiled abstractedly at someone who had waved at her from a nearby table. We were seated at a discreet corner table, the better to discuss business with our guests.

'I told Nova. Lucy wasn't answering the phone.'

'Then where are they?' Evangeline hadn't stopped watching the door since we'd arrived. 'It's half past one.' And, since we had arrived early, we were on our second sherry; the sherries we had ordered for Lucy and Nova waited at the place settings.

'Maybe their car broke down. Or they ran out of petrol.' Or maybe they'd changed their minds, but I'd hold back that explanation for another half an hour. If they hadn't shown by then, Evangeline might be better able to accept it.

'Why don't we go ahead and order the first course?' I had nibbled everything in sight

231

except the flowers. 'I'm starving. I don't think they'd mind.' I didn't think they'd even notice. If they came. I remembered the curious note in Nova's voice and the reluctance with which she'd agreed that Lucy would love to lunch at the Ivy. Ordinarily.

'We'll give them ten more minutes.' Evangeline toyed with the slim sheaf of pages she had placed beside her plate. If she kept on, they'd be dog-eared. Thank heavens there was no way to tell they'd been photocopied.

Most of the other diners were making their selections from the sweet trolley before Nova finally appeared in the entrance. She had made an effort, I'll say that for her. She wasn't wearing the baseball cap and her wraparound skirt might have needed ironing, but it was a gesture in the right direction, as was the slightly too-tight ruffled blouse in a style I hadn't seen for years.

'But where's Lucy?' Evangeline looked beyond Nova, but there was no one else in sight.

'My dear, how nice to see you.' Her smile was strained as she greeted Nova. 'And how ... nice you look.'

'Lucy isn't coming.' Nova wasted no time on the preliminaries. 'She's still furious. I just wanted to let you know. I'll go now. I know she's the one you really want to see.'

'Not so fast.' I caught her wrist and pulled her back. 'Sit down. We invited you both to lunch. I'm afraid we *did* order our appetizers, but have your sherry and look at the menu.'

'You mean it? Thanks.' She sat down, rocking the table as she knocked against it, and caught up the glass of sherry as though it were a lifeline. 'I'm sorry to be so late. I've been arguing with Lu, but I just can't budge her. She gets awfully stubborn when she's mad.'

She took a deep quaff from the glass and I surreptitiously nudged the untouched glass intended for Lucy nearer to her. She looked as though she needed it.

The waiter responded instantly to our desperate signals and Evangeline relaxed slightly as Nova ordered from the set lunch.

'I'm sorry Lucy is so upset.' It was as close to an apology as Evangeline was likely to get. 'Tell me, my dear, what can I do to make amends?'

'I ... I don't know. She's worse than usual.' The way Nova was avoiding all eye contact was making me uneasy. 'I've never seen her like this before.'

'But she usually gets over it?' Evangeline was growing uneasy, too.

'Usually ...' The waiter set Nova's soup down before her and she dived into it with relief. Now she could avoid talking, as well as eye contact.

But you can't make soup last for ever and, when she surfaced, with only a few more spots on her ruffles, Evangeline was still waiting.

'What are her favourite flowers?'

'Umm...' Nova found something very interesting to look at on the far wall. 'I ... I wouldn't bother with any more flowers, if I were you. The ones you sent ... Well, I fished them out of the wastebasket and they're in my room now. I hope you don't mind.'

'Not at all.' Evangeline's jawline tightened. 'Did she throw everything else away, too?'

'She wanted to, but we wouldn't let her. She fed most of the tea cakes and biscuits to Tex. And the others took care of the liquor. Lucy *did* eat most of the chocolates herself,' she added consolingly.

'What others?' Evangeline pounced.

'Those ... Irishmen!' Nova spoke with some venom. 'They're underfoot all the time now. And ... and...' She looked away unhappily. 'Lucy gave me a message for you. But I don't want to tell you ... I don't want to believe it myself...'

Uh-oh. I exchanged glances with Evangeline.

'Come along,' Evangeline encouraged. 'It can't be as bad as you think. Lucy will have to come round eventually. And I still—' She smiled with the triumph of one who held the upper hand. 'I still have the script—and I insist on returning it to her myself. Personally.'

'That's just it.' Nova sniffled. 'She says you can keep it! She isn't interested any more.'

'What?' Evangeline paled. She had two-thirds of a first act; without the rest of the play, it was useless.

'She can't mean it,' I said.

'She can! She does!' Nova took an unsteady breath. 'That ... that ... *Irishman* ... got at her. She's hypnotized by him! They're going to collaborate! They're going to write an Epic Poem about an ancient Celtic King of Ireland and his noble ... *damned!* ... Irish wolfhound!'

I snatched the plate out of her way just in time.

She hurled herself forward on to the table, burying her head in her forearms and burst into loud howling sobs.

Evangeline shuddered. 'Thank heavens we didn't go to the Savoy,' she murmured.

*   *   *

We dried Nova's tears, listened to her fears, got her fed and, eventually, got rid of her.

It didn't help our dispositions to find Nigel hovering in the entrance hall when we got back to base.

'Ah! Ah, good!' He darted forward, blocking our path to the lifts. 'I was hoping to run into you. I'd, ah, like a word with you.'

'Yes?' We paused and looked at him impatiently.

'Ah!' He shifted from one foot to the other and back again. 'A word with *you*,' he repeated, looking pointedly at Evangeline.

235

'Don't mind me.' I can take a hint. I began to move away. 'I'll see you later. I'd like to lie down for a bit, anyway.'

'Are you all right?' Nigel's voice rose with alarm. 'There's nothing wrong?'

'No, but I haven't felt quite right since the other night. Being half asphyxiated, first by smoke, then by strangulation, doesn't really do anything to improve your digestion. I've had, I guess you could call it, a nervous stomach ever since.' And perhaps I had eaten a bit too much at the Ivy, but I wasn't going to admit that.

'Ah! Yes!' Nigel did not look much the happier for my explanation. 'I see. Get some rest. Best thing, probably.'

'I knew you shouldn't have had those profiteroles,' Evangeline was quick to criticize. 'And, as for having cream on top—' She shuddered. 'You've brought it on yourself.'

I began walking away while she was still pointing out my iniquities. Just before I got out of earshot, I heard Nigel say: 'I've had a rather odd telephone call from Ledbetter...'

*　　　*　　　*

I must have fallen asleep. When I opened my eyes, it was dark outside. After a long moment, I became aware of a motionless figure silhouetted in the doorway, staring at me. That was what had disturbed my rest.

'Evangeline?' I sat up and blinked. The

236

figure became recognizable. 'Evangeline, what is it?'

'I didn't mean to wake you.' She snapped the light on, completing the job. 'But, since you're awake anyway...'

'What time is it?' I hadn't meant to fall asleep. I had intended to close my eyes for just a minute or two, then call Martha and arrange to get together with the children.

'Six o'clock,' Evangeline said. 'I thought it would be better to let you sleep until we were ready.'

'Ready for what?' I looked at her with suspicion. 'The last I heard, we didn't have any plans for tonight.'

'Mmm, yes. That's been changed, I'm afraid. Time is flying, after all, and I thought we should take a look at the revised *Gather Ye Rosebuds* at the Happy Larry as soon as possible. Tonight, if you're feeling up to it.'

'I'm OK.' All the better for having had a nap, but still a bit puzzled. 'What did Nigel have to say?'

'Several very interesting things.' She turned away. 'He's calling Ledbetter to let the club know we'll see them there tonight.'

'Do we have to? I really enjoyed that lunchtime theatre when they weren't around.'

'We'll keep them at a distance. Nigel will escort us—and I've also invited Terence. He's flying to Los Angeles tomorrow with ... with Sweetums. It will cheer him to have some

237

company and see a show tonight.'

'Considering it's where Sweetums died— and even the same show—I doubt that it's going to cheer him very much.' Honestly, sometimes Evangeline could be so obtuse.

'Even so, it will be better for him than sitting home alone and brooding.' Evangeline had no doubts. 'He said so himself. He quite jumped at the invitation.'

Oh, well, if it wasn't going to bother him, why should I feel sensitive on his behalf? Maybe she had a point.

'And...' she added with elaborate casualness ... 'Ron will meet us there.'

'Ron?' It took me a moment to remember. 'You mean Superintendent Heyhoe?'

'It *is* his local,' she said innocently. Too innocently.

'Evangeline, what are you up to?'

'Nothing. Nothing at all. Now hurry up and get changed, if you're going to.' She turned again and clumped from the room.

Clumped? I got up and followed her, staring incredulously at her feet. She appeared to be shod in ungainly lumps that were a cross between black trainers and old-fashioned diving boots—the sort they strapped on the diver just before the great heavy helmet was lowered on to his head and he went down to collect the sunken treasure on the sea bed, only to have to fight to the death with the giant octopus he found guarding it.

'Evangeline, what the hell have you got on your feet?'

'Doc Martens.' She lifted each foot, with some difficulty, for my inspection. 'All the rage. Do you like them?'

'They don't really do anything for you.'

'Don't they?' She regarded them absently. 'Give them time. I think they'll do a lot.'

'Evangeline—' The last time I'd seen her in anything like that was in *Klara of the Klondike*, when she strapped on her lover's diving boots and stomped in to wreck the saloon where the baddies had stolen all his money in a crooked poker game.

'Evangeline, you're *not* going to wear those tonight!'

'They have to be broken in,' she said. 'I wouldn't dream of taking them off now.'

*   *   *

'Welcome! Welcome!' Barry Lane came forward to greet our party as we entered the Happy Larry. I noticed that his handclasp with Evangeline was prolonged and he looked straight into her eyes, nodding for emphasis as an unspoken message passed between them.

'Ron will be a little late,' he said, 'but he'll definitely be here by the interval.'

'The interval.' Terence gave a deep sigh. This pub did not hold the happiest of memories for him—and the interval had provided the worst memory.

'You're sure you wouldn't like a bite to eat before the show?' Barry asked. 'I'll fix it myself.'

'Thanks, but I'm not hungry,' I said.

'After that lunch, I should think not,' Evangeline said. 'Nor am I. I warned Nigel to eat before we left—'

'Ah! Quite!' Nigel agreed. 'Full! Couldn't manage another mouthful.'

'Unless Terence—?' Evangeline looked at him.

'No, no.' He blanched. 'I couldn't. Not here. Oh, no offence,' he assured Barry hastily. 'But . . .' He looked at the stairs. 'Not here.'

'Of course, of course.' Barry took no offence. 'I understand. A drink, perhaps?'

'Later,' Evangeline said, looking beyond him. 'I see everyone is here.'

'Oh, no question of that. You've got quite a claque there. Every single one of them told me you'd be coming tonight. I didn't let on that I already knew.'

'Good.' Evangeline waved absently to the young men, but turned away as they started towards us, Greg and Adam in the lead.

'I think we'll go straight upstairs and get good seats. Come along, Terence.' Evangeline took his arm as Sweetums had once done.

'Just a minute.' At the foot of the stairs, Terence stopped. For a moment, I thought he would go no farther, but that wasn't what he

240

had in mind.

'It was right here—' His voice broke. 'This ... very ... spot.' He reached up and removed the white carnation from his buttonhole. Head bowed, he solemnly dropped the carnation on to the spot where Sweetums had lain. Where Sweetums had died.

The gesture halted Adam and Greg in their tracks. The others piled up behind them. They sorted themselves out and began backing away. This was too graphic a reminder of what had happened here.

'Shall we continue?' Terence offered his arm to Evangeline again. They circled around the carnation and ascended the stairs, the dignity of the occasion only slightly marred by the clumping of Evangeline's Doc Martens. I hoped I was the only one to notice.

I took Nigel's arm, since he seemed to expect it, and we started up the stairs behind them. Something hard and oddly shaped in his jacket pocket bumped against me sharply. Another bruise, I supposed. What was one more amongst so many?

'Are we going backstage?' It would be a while before the show started. I didn't see why we couldn't have waited downstairs.

'Afterwards, perhaps.' Evangeline was fully occupied in deciding the best place to sit. 'Or perhaps not. Not for long, anyway. Just long enough to invite that nice girl and her genius boyfriend to lunch with us at the

241

Ivy tomorrow.'

'If they ever let us in again,' I muttered.

Disregarding me, Evangeline chose a row and waved Terence forward. Nigel stepped back to let me go ahead of him.

Oddly, we wound up with Evangeline and me in the middle, Terence and Nigel on the outside on either side, rather than the usual mixed seating. No one else seemed to think it odd, however, so I dismissed it with a mental shrug. Perhaps Evangeline had had enough of Nigel.

The few musicians who were masquerading as an orchestra took their places and began playing. It couldn't be called an overture; it was a medley of songs from the show interspersed with some old standards. If it weren't for the new original numbers, I could have grown quite nostalgic. As it was, I was conscious of a faint rising excitement. Maybe something was going to come of this, after all. If the writers couldn't come up with something quite right, surely Hugh would know a good play doctor who could work on the material. Evangeline was right: Hugh *had* been neglecting us lately.

The room was filling up now and there was a buzz of activity in the wings. I heard the bell sound in the distance and felt quite smug at being comfortably settled in my seat for a change.

On the second bell, the Open and Shut Club

242

straggled in. Greg and Ledbetter came over to us, each carrying a drink in both hands.

'Something to see you through the first act.' Greg handed brandy snifters containing double measures to Evangeline and me. Ledbetter—somewhat grudgingly, I thought—presented Terence and Nigel with half-pints of beer.

'How kind,' Evangeline cooed. A corner of her mouth twitched.

'Ah! Thanks!' Nigel looked at his as though wondering what to do with it. I realized I had never seen him drink anything so plebeian as beer.

'See you at the interval.' Greg and Ledbetter went off to the seats their friends were saving for them.

As I raised the glass to my lips, I felt a tug at my elbow.

'Don't drink it!' Evangeline said ventriloquially.

Startled, I turned to look at her. All her attention seemed to be centred raptly on the stage. She spoke again without moving her lips: 'Pretend to sip it. When the lights go down, pass it to Nigel.'

What on earth? I kept my own face blank and did as directed. The liquid sloshed around in my glass; no one watching could tell that I hadn't swallowed any of it. Evangeline did the same.

Beside me, Nigel put his hand in his pocket,

not withdrawing it until the lights went down. Then he swiftly placed his glass of beer on the floor and used both hands to hold and uncap a small bottle. When I gave him my glass, he poured the contents into the bottle, recapped it and replaced it in his pocket.

On the other side of Evangeline, Terence was doing the same with her drink. The show had started, but I was too bemused to have any interest in it.

Had paranoia finally set in? Or did Evangeline know something I didn't know?

CHAPTER NINETEEN

The first act flew past and, despite my misgivings, I got caught up in it. The skits had been tightened up, the new songs were funny and poignant, the pace of the whole thing was faster and I blinked in disbelief when the lights went up.

The Open and Shutters moved towards us purposefully, but Cara Knowlton got there first.

'Barry told us you'd be here tonight,' she said. 'Please come backstage and have a drink.' She giggled unexpectedly. 'He's even supplied the champagne.'

'We'd be delighted.' Evangeline led as we followed Cara beyond the curtain to the region

244

where the uninvited dared not tread. I caught a glimpse of disgruntled faces behind us as the curtain cut us off from them. Too bad, boys, we'll see you after the show—if we can't avoid it.

As the champagne splashed into my glass, I glanced at Evangeline questioningly. She nodded agreement, so I sipped my first drink of the evening. The cast clustered round us. Terence and Nigel were having a wonderful time and I was enjoying it myself. Evangeline made the date for the Ivy tomorrow and, all too soon, the interval had ended and we were back in our seats.

The second act wasn't quite as good as the first but, as everyone had assured us, they were still working on it. Or maybe part of the problem was that prickly feeling I was getting at the back of my neck, the sensation you get when you're being secretly observed.

I rubbed my hand across the nape of my neck and looked over my shoulder. Everyone seemed to be watching the stage and yet I got the impression that someone's gaze had just shifted.

'Are you all right?' Evangeline whispered.

'I guess so.' Definitely, no one had me under observation now. The strong sensation had gone, but left a lingering aftermath. I kept wanting to look over my shoulder and catch those staring hostile eyes.

'It won't be much longer,' Evangeline said.

'Nearly over now.'

Somehow, that failed to cheer me. I realized that I didn't want to leave the refuge of my seat and walk down those stairs—those deadly stairs. And ... wasn't there a faint mocking scent of heliotrope in the air? Perhaps because Terence was with us, Sweetums suddenly seemed very close.

That didn't cheer me, either. We had always made a point of keeping a good distance from Sweetums in life; I certainly didn't want to be close to her now.

The storm of enthusiastic applause lifted us from our seats in a standing ovation. There might still be work to be done on the show, but the audience at the Happy Larry had no doubt that they were present at the birth of a hit.

'Terrific, wasn't it?' Adam and the others surrounded us as we remained in our seats, waiting for the audience to file out. 'Too bad the Sylvesters couldn't make it. I'm sure they would have loved it.'

'Perhaps they'll come another night,' Greg said hopefully.

'I fear not.' Evangeline dashed his hopes. 'Beau and Juanita have gone back to their home in the country. They won't be visiting Town again for quite some time.'

'Oh.' I knew Adam had a thing about Juanita, but I was surprised to see Greg look so disappointed.

'Come and have a drink with us.' A friendly

hand on my shoulder usually doesn't make me jump, but tonight it did. I turned sharply and Ledbetter snatched his hand away as though I'd slapped it.

That crawling feeling had returned to the nape of my neck and was inching down my spine.

'You boys go ahead,' Evangeline said. 'We'll be along in a minute.'

They seemed obscurely dissatisfied by this decision but, as we remained seated and Evangeline embarked on a low-voiced, obviously private conversation with Terence, they had to accept it.

'Nigel,' I said, 'what's happening? Why have you got my drink in your pocket?'

'Ah! Good question!' he said and lapsed into a brooding silence.

'Well,' I prompted, 'what's the answer?'

'What, indeed? Orders! Just following orders.' He nodded at Evangeline.

'The stairs should be clear now.' Evangeline rose. 'Shall we join the ... gentlemen?'

She led the way. Although the staircase was deserted, Nigel and Terence remained protectively by our sides. Looking down, I could see that the Open and Shutters had claimed a large table in a corner and were watching our progress, gesturing for us to join them. Again, I had the sensation that someone was watching me intently. Too intently.

'You seem to be Flavour of the Month,

247

Trixie.' Evangeline had noticed it, too. 'Star of the Show. So why don't you give them a show?'

'There's no music here,' I pointed out. 'What do you want me to do—slide down the banister?'

'A simple death scene will suffice. Give the audience what it wants.'

'Now, listen—' The look in her eyes stopped me cold. She wasn't kidding.

The carnation was still in place at the foot of the stairs, neither trodden on nor kicked aside. Everyone had respectfully walked around it, recognizing its sinister implication. I stared at it, mesmerized. Was it my imagination that the scent of heliotrope seemed to waft upwards from it?

Evangeline stepped off the last stair, swerved around the carnation and turned to look at me.

'Sway!' she directed, sotto voce. 'Clutch at your stomach. You're an actress—act!'

'Ooooh . . .' I moaned. Swaying came easily. I really felt dizzy as I began to put a few clues together. Nigel gave me a furtive push, so that I sagged against the banister.

'OH, NO!' Terence was no actor, but he made up for it in volume. 'NOT HERE! NOT AGAIN!'

'Trixie, speak to me!' Evangeline moved in to try to steal my scene. '*Trixie!*'

The Open and Shutters charged across the room in a body to crowd around me. Some of the regular patrons moved forward, others backed away, not wanting to get involved. A

248

few left.

'Oooooh!' Now was the moment, I judged, to fold both arms across my stomach and double up. I collapsed on the last stair and leaned against the stair-rail.

'Stand back! Give her air!' Barry Lane pushed his way to my side.

'Trixie!' Evangeline's cry was a model of anguish. Through half-closed eyes, I saw her make a curious shaking movement of one hand. Drops of a clear liquid scattered across the floor and the smell of heliotrope became overwhelming. Several people recoiled without realizing why.

'The back room!' Barry Lane lifted me expertly. 'Get her into the snug. You'—he glared at Nigel—'call an ambulance!'

'Yes! Right!' Nigel moved away, but not very far. In the distance, I could see Superintendent Heyhoe hovering. A couple of very businesslike-looking men in plain clothes were with him.

The Open and Shutters surrounded us as Barry carried me to a private room at the back. I had opted for keeping my eyes closed now, but I could hear suitable exclamations of shock and distress coming from the various members.

'What happened? Did she fall?'

'Air! Give her air!'

'Is there a doctor in the house?' That was Vic—and the most practical question I had heard yet. There wasn't, of course. Like policemen, there never is when you need one. Except ... Heyhoe was already there and waiting.

'No one else!' Barry ordered over his shoulder as he carried me through the doorway. 'Keep them out!'

Nigel and Terence blocked the doorway. They pushed the others back as they tried to follow us, and slammed the door in their faces. Then they leaned their backs against the door and exchanged grim nods.

'So far, so good.' Barry dumped me into a chair. 'How long, do you think? And how about a drink while we're waiting? We've earned it.' He moved to a small bar in the corner and began pouring.

'The other drinks were poisoned,' I said to Evangeline. 'Is that it?'

'Probably,' she said, 'and not for the first time. I knew that eggnog wouldn't have reacted on me the way it seemed to. It was what I'd had at the pub beforehand. And you're too tough to let a bit of smoke and a mauling affect you the way they did.'

'I thought that steak-and-kidney pie was terrible,' I recalled. 'But I put it down to lousy cooking and cheap ingredients.'

'And, I'm afraid, a little extra something sprinkled over the top before it reached you.'

'But why?' We accepted our drinks from Barry and took long swallows. 'Why on earth

250

should anyone want to kill us?'

'That was what I couldn't understand until'—Evangeline flashed him a smile—'dear Nigel explained the Bad Taste Sweepstakes to me.'

'Bad Taste Sweepstakes?' I seemed to have heard that name before. 'You mean the pool the Open and Shutters were running?'

'*Are* running.' Evangeline looked thoughtful. 'No wonder they wouldn't let me join in their little game.'

'Evangeline, if you don't tell me what—'

She stood up and let out an anguished scream.

That silenced all conversation in the room—and outside in the saloon bar, too.

'Trixie!' she screamed in agonized tones, moving over to stand in front of the door and pitching her voice to reach the other side.

'No! *No!* Trixie! *Come back!* Trixie!' She gave way to wild sobbing noises.

'Thank you very much.' I looked at her incredulously. 'Now what do I do for an encore?'

She opened the door a couple of inches. The deep uneasy silence outside was suddenly broken by the loud pop of a champagne cork. The same sound we had heard just as Sweetums died.

Evangeline quietly closed the door with an expression of grim satisfaction.

251

'You lose somebody quite a lot of money,' she said.

* * *

We finished our drinks slowly, almost reluctantly. I didn't ask any more questions. I was going to find out soon enough.

There was a soft tap at the door and Superintendent Heyhoe entered. He nodded at Evangeline. 'We've got him dead to rights,' he said. 'Bring her out and let's finish it off.'

'Come along, Trixie.' Evangeline stood up and waved me forward. 'This is your encore.'

I'd never made an entrance like that in my life before. But I'd never played the Skeleton at the Feast before. I walked slowly through the saloon bar, with each table and each group of people falling silent as I passed it. Evangeline and Superintendent Heyhoe walked immediately behind me, one at each shoulder.

From the looks on the faces watching us, we must have exuded a considerable air of menace. The Last Chance Gang heading for a shoot-out.

Ledbetter, sitting, as usual, with his back to the wall, was the first of that group to look up and see us. See me. All colour drained from his face. His mouth opened, but no sound came out.

One by one, the others looked at him, then turned to see what had had such a devastating effect on him. It devastated them, too.

252

Never before had my sweetest smile engendered such shock and horror. They were all speechless. I thought Greg might faint.

'The report of my death was greatly exaggerated.' I had always wanted to use that line.

'You're going to have to give it all back, you know.' Evangeline used a more pragmatic line.

'Time, gentlemen, please.' Barry took the curtain line. 'We're closing now. Time, gentlemen, please.'

*   *   *

'This one got the payoff.' The policeman's hand descended on Greg's shoulder.

'And I believe Mr Ledbetter is deep in the conspiracy also,' Evangeline said. 'He's been remarkably assiduous in his telephoning. Too much so for a disinterested party.'

'Telephoned me,' Nigel agreed. 'Out of the blue. Always wanting to make sure I'd bring you to certain pubs on certain nights.'

'And you weren't the only one. After that first unfortunate scene at the Drawbridge, when he realized Dorsal Finn bore rather a lot of animosity towards us, he added Dorsal to his telephone list, didn't you, Ledbetter?'

Evangeline paused, but Ledbetter just stared at her stonily. He was not about to be tricked into any incriminating admissions.

'He telephoned Dorsal Finn to tip him off

253

that we were going to be at the Queen and Country the other night in the hope of making mischief. He must have felt that he'd succeeded beyond his wildest hopes when Dorsal actually attacked Trixie in front of witnesses. After that, he thought he was safe, no matter what he did. It was simply a case of ensuring that Dorsal turned up at the Wounded Lion on the night he intended to push Trixie off the balcony. Everyone knew that Dorsal had already tried to kill her once. If there was any suspicion that the fall from the balcony was deliberate murder, Dorsal was on the scene and ready-made for the role of Suspect Number One.'

'Murder?' Vic stared from Greg to Ledbetter, aghast. 'What are you talking about?'

'About certain of your friends who have been adding their own embellishments to your little game,' Evangeline said. 'Nasty ones—for a nasty game. When you're betting on lives with the wrong sort of people you're also risking those lives. Greed is a powerful motivator.'

'The Bad Taste Sweepstakes,' Nigel said. 'They've got one going in every pub around town, not just here. Lots of money involved. Very bad form.'

'Keep talking,' I said. 'I think I'm entitled to a full explanation—especially as I seem to be intimately involved.'

'Ah!' Nigel winced and avoided my eyes. 'Pub games, you see. All sorts. Betting, mostly: darts, horses, greyhounds, cards—fine. People—' He frowned. 'That's why it's bad taste. Betting on who'll die first. Take all those celebrities in the public eye who aren't so young any more, or who've announced illnesses, or who just live dangerously. Royals, of course, plenty of ancient ones, plus the odd chance of an assassination. Then all the stars of sports, theatre, opera, ballet, politics—the field is endless, lots of elderly prospects. Names in a hat and pull 'em out. When the name you hold goes, you've won the Sweeps and everyone builds up the stake again for the next one. Not very nice. Especially if you help them along. Not fair. Not playing the game.'

'And Greg held *my* name?' I was feeling dizzy again.

'They invited me to join in.' Nigel was looking everywhere except at Evangeline and me. 'Then began making noises about how close I was to the two of you. Whether you might be accident-prone. Odd little insinuations. Made me uneasy. Began to smell a rat—'

'This is bloody ridiculous!' Greg blustered. 'What if I did hold her name? It may be bad taste—but it's not illegal.'

'Anyway,' Ledbetter found his tongue. 'Trixie isn't dead. She isn't even harmed. You've got nothing to complain about. It was

255

all a mistake.'

'Your mistake.' Evangeline looked from one to the other. 'Sweetums Carew is dead.' Again the faint smell of heliotrope wafted across the scene as Evangeline pointed at them accusingly.

'You held *her* name, Ledbetter.' Adam looked dazed. 'And you were on the stairs when she fell. Is this true?'

'What about you?' Ledbetter counterattacked. 'You made a packet when Gervaise Cordwainer snuffed it.'

'*Sir* Gervaise,' Evangeline pointed out coldly, 'was ninety-six and died naturally. That is more than can be said for Sweetums Carew.'

'I'll have to ask you all to come along to the station and help us with our inquiries,' Superintendent Heyhoe announced.

'Don't say anything!' Greg warned as Ledbetter opened his mouth to protest. Greg swung about to face Heyhoe. 'We're not saying another word until our legal representative is with us.'

'Certainly, sir,' Heyhoe agreed coldly. 'That's your right. You can call him from the station.'

Silently, Greg got to his feet. As he walked past Evangeline, she stuck out her foot and tripped him. As he fell, her foot moved again.

'She kicked me!' He hit the ground howling, his vow of silence forgotten.

'You tried to kill Trixie!' She kicked him

256

again. Those Doc Martens were doing something for her, after all.

'Stop her!' he howled to Heyhoe. 'She's trying to kill me!'

'Turnabout is fair play,' I told him.

'You tried to kill *me!*' Evangeline's foot was a blur. This time there was a strange snapping noise.

'My leg! My leg! She's broken my leg! You're the police—stop her. She's broken my leg!'

'Really, sir?' Heyhoe looked around the room, looked everywhere except at Evangeline. 'I hadn't noticed a thing.' He looked at Nigel and Terence. 'Any of you see anything untoward?'

Evangeline kicked again. The kicks were creeping closer to Greg's head.

'Evangeline—' I warned. She was likely to get carried away.

'We're waiting for you, sir,' Heyhoe said to Ledbetter who, not surprisingly, was reluctant to walk past Evangeline.

'Come along, Ledbetter.' She bared her teeth at him. 'You're not afraid of a little kick, are you? It won't hurt nearly as much as if you'd dashed your brains out on cobblestones.'

'I do sympathize, madam,' Heyhoe said. 'But please desist now. The newspapers blame *us* when the suspects are duffed up.'

'Evangeline,' I said, 'that's enough.' But she had reminded me vividly of that endless

257

terrifying flight through thin air.

Somehow, I found Vic's heavy pint beer mug in my hand. I crashed it down on Ledbetter's head—it seemed the right place for it. Ledbetter slumped to the floor with a satisfactory thud and I saw Evangeline plant a neat one in his ribs.

'Oh, Gawd!' Heyhoe moaned. 'And they'll call it police brutality.'

* * *

For some reason, Superintendent Heyhoe didn't want us in the police van with the Open and Shut Club. He didn't even want us in the same police station with them. He cravenly muttered something about calling on us in the morning for our statements as he led everyone away.

We stayed on with Terence and Nigel to have a quiet after-hours drink with Barry.

'You know, Trixie'—Evangeline sipped at her brandy—'I'm a little afraid that we might have been a teensy bit responsible for Ledbetter's actions.'

'Us?' I squeaked. 'How could we be?'

'We were too polite,' she said.

I choked on my drink.

'Yes, Trixie. Instead of simply walking out of those dreadful shows, we tried to spare the actors' feelings by taking turns pretending to be ill. It must have given Ledbetter the impression that we had the proverbial one foot in the grave and the other on a banana skin. He thought he could get away with giving us a push to help us along.'

'He'd have killed anyway, sooner or later,' I said. 'After all, he started with Sweetums and there was nothing wrong with her. Physically, that is—' I broke off with an anxious sidelong glance at Terence.

'That's right,' Terence said. 'And I would like to say how grateful I am to you for letting me help to bring those dastards to justice. Only . . .' he looked at Evangeline uneasily. 'I still feel a trifle guilty about taking that perfume out of Sweetums's personal effects— they were entrusted to me to return to her family. Oh, I know it was in a good cause—I could see how the scent of heliotrope helped to unnerve those men—but that was a very rare perfume. Sweetums told me it had been created especially for her. I hope her family will understand . . .'

'Don't worry.' I cut across Evangeline's snort. I should have known where Evangeline got that perfume. Poor Terence, he was putty in her hands. Like so many others.

'Her family won't mind at all.' I could guarantee it. Anyone who had ever met Sweetums had learned to hate the scent of heliotrope. The aversion must have been doubled in spades for her family. He'd just saved them the trouble of throwing the stuff

259

away. But it wouldn't really be tactful to tell him that.

'By giving Evangeline that perfume to use, you helped enormously,' I assured him. 'You can face her family with a clear conscience.'

'Well...' He brightened. 'I do feel I've done a little something towards avenging Sweetums—and I'm grateful to you for giving me the opportunity.'

'Ah! Right!' Nigel said. 'Agreed! Nothing I could have done about ... about ... my own problem. But I don't feel quite so useless now. If, ah, there's anything else I can ever do...'

'How very kind,' Evangeline cooed. 'Perhaps you wouldn't mind escorting us to the occasional show in the evening. Since you seem to be acquiring a taste for the theatre.'

'Ah! Always liked the theatre. Runs in the family.' He beamed. 'My uncle owns one. Great-uncle, that is. Theatre, that is.'

'Owns a theatre?' Evangeline's hands curled into predatory talons and hovered over Nigel's arm. 'Which one?'

'Ah! You wouldn't know it. Hasn't been open in years. Decades. "Dark", they say, don't they? Pity. Perfectly preserved little Victorian gem under some railway arches.'

'Evangeline—' I warned.

'The prospect of a theatre, Trixie,' she breathed. 'An available theatre! At last.'

'Why has it been closed for so long?' I wanted to know. 'Especially if it's such a gem?'

260

'Ah! Sad. Very sad. Uncle won't let anyone use it. Tragedy of his life. His sweetheart committed suicide there. Kept it as a shrine ever since. Not that anyone's been too anxious to get it. Haunted, they say.'

'Yes,' I said gloomily. 'It would be.' We had lacked only that.

'We'll talk about this later,' Evangeline said, not giving up for a minute. 'When we're not so tired.'

'Evangeline—'

'Time to go home...' She set down her glass and stretched like a cat, a predatory gleam in her eye as she smiled at Nigel. 'Dear Ron will be visiting us in the morning and...' She sent me a conspiratorial wink...

'And I'm just dying to ask him who was holding Cecile Savoy's name.'

261

We hope you have enjoyed this Large Print book. Other Chivers Press or G.K. Hall & Co. Large Print books are available at your library or directly from the publishers.

For more information about current and forthcoming titles, please call or write, without obligation, to:

Chivers Press Limited
Windsor Bridge Road
Bath BA2 3AX
England
Tel. (01225) 335336

OR

G.K. Hall & Co.
P.O. Box 159
Thorndike, Maine 04986
USA
Tel. (800) 223–2336

All our Large Print titles are designed for easy reading, and all our books are made to last.